FREAKY FROGS

To Fano,
Frogs are
important!
Bonnie C

FREAKY FROGS

BONNIE T. OGLE

Fired Up Press
Newberry, Florida

Published by Fired Up Press
Newberry, Florida

ISBN 978-1-7340500-0-4

Typesetting services by BOOKOW.COM

For my favorite herpetologists

Morgan Joy
Miranda Noelle
Jackson Edward
Raina Glory

Contents

Chapter 1

New Neighbors

JACKSON parted the brush and peered at the rocks, looking for frogs. He immediately saw one. On this relatively warm day in May, the sun heated the rocks enough that a frog or two could be found warming themselves from the radiant heat, after a swim in the cold creek. "Ah, there you are!" he whispered softly, wielding his dip net. He was an old hand at catching frogs, usually with his bare hands.

This one, however, sat on a rock about a foot from the shoreline, presenting more of a challenge. Jackson didn't want to overreach and slip on the muddy bank, something he'd done more than once. The net gave him an advantage.

"Alright, Buggy Eyes, I know you can see a pretty wide range, but I'm smarter than you." He sneaked up behind it and lowered the net. Whap! "Gotcha!" He grabbed the net and the frog's hind legs and carried it to his portable habitat. "Hold still, now. It'll be easier to get you out of this thing. Your big brothers never seem to get it." Removing the frog from the net, Jackson said, "Well, that was easy. Now let's see if you're a boy or a girl." Flipping it over onto his palm, he noted the brown chin. "Ah, a boy!"

He tossed the frog into the habitat, and started back home. Jackson's house was near the creek, in an area of homes built on what had once been a ranch. Trudging across the lawn, Jackson noticed his neighbor, Dr. Thomson, sitting on his back step, a glass of purple liquid in his hand. He wore a large, floppy hat which covered his eyes, so he had to raise his head to see.

Jackson smiled to himself, thinking, *Kind of looks like Mom's garden hat.* That was Dr. T., always practical. The doctor had a small pail hooked to his belt. Jackson had seen him take a handful of berries out of the pail and throw not one, but two berries into the air and catch them both in his mouth!

He knew his friend worked with animals at the University, but he wondered if he worked with plants, too. More than once, he had seen his friend snipping bits off various plants in the yard and dropping them into the pail. *There sure are a lot of unusual plants in Dr. Thomson's yard.* At first glance, the yard appeared unkempt, but the more time Jackson spent there, the more he realized there was an order to the place.

Jackson stopped. Hesitating, he looked down at his captive. As if talking to the frog, he said, "Dr. T. is really funny, but he's a busy man. A busy, smart man."

"Hello, neighbor! How about a glass of acai berry juice?" the doctor asked. "It'll keep you young. Full of antioxidants!" Jackson smiled and shook his head, heading towards his neighbor. *You never know what Dr. Thomson will come up with next,* Jackson thought. *Why would I want to stay young?*

"So, what have you got there?" Dr. Thomson asked. Jackson held the small container up for him to see.

"Ah, a sentinel! Jackson, what's green and hops?"

"Huh? A frog?" said Jackson.

"Right-o. What's red and hops?"

Jackson waited for the answer.

"A very angry frog," Dr. Thomson said. "What's green and dangerous?"

"I know it's some kind of frog," Jackson answered, smiling. Dr. Thomson was confusing sometimes, but always fun and Jackson usually learned something new when they were together.

"Yep. A frog with a hand grenade." Jackson grimaced.

" So, let's have a look at your green hopper."

As the two peered at the frog through the clear sides of the carrier, Jackson asked, "What did you call him, Dr. T.? I mean, besides red, angry, and dangerous."

"A sentinel," Dr. Thomson answered.

"I've never heard of that species."

Now it was Dr. Thomson's turn to smile. "It's not a species. Many frogs and toads are sentinels." Jackson's eyes crinkled as he looked into his older friend's face.

"A sentinel is a guard or a lookout who gives a warning when danger appears."

"I don't get it. How can a frog or toad give a warning? I've heard of soldiers guarding camp, blowing a horn to wake everyone. But frogs …" His face lit up, "Oh, I get it! Their croaking."

"Well, their croaking is a means of communication. But the warning amphibians give to humans has quite a different manifestation. You know they have permeable skin. It soaks up whatever is in water. And if there's a harmful chemical in the water…"

"Oh, I see!" Jackson spoke slowly, looking down towards his feet. "If there's poison in the water, it'll kill the frogs before people notice it." He looked up at Dr. Thomson.

"You got it. Did you ever hear of the canary in the coal mine?" Dr. Thomson continued, "Before they had sophisticated equipment to monitor air quality in mines, the men took a canary down with them. Why do you think they did that?"

Jackson's mouth opened wide. "So the canary would warn them if the air was bad!" He was quiet for a moment. "But wouldn't the bird die?"

Dr. Thomson was quiet, watching his young friend.

"Oh, I know. The canary was a sentinel."

Dr. Thomson nodded.

Dr. T. is always using big words, Jackson thought. *I like that. He makes me feel like an equal instead of a kid, even if I don't know what he's talking about.*

"Say, Jackson. Why are frogs such liars?"

"Huh?"

"Frogs are liars because they're am-**phib**-ians." Dr. Thomson lowered his head, looking at Jackson, who slowly smiled. The two sat on a step, watching the sun lower behind the trees at the far end of the yard. They heard a few frogs, and some chirping crickets. Jackson thought about the sentinels and why a frog would want to give a warning. "Dr. T., What's a frog's favorite car?"

"Hmmm. Tell me. What's a frog's favorite car?"

"A beetle."

Dr. Thomson slapped his knee. "Good one!" Jackson was glad his older friend liked his joke.

A light rain began to fall. "Well, good night, Dr. T. Dad will be looking for me to help with dinner. It's our night to cook and give Mom a break."

"A lucky lady. Good night, my young herpetologist. Tell the folks I said hello."

Jackson waved as he headed to the back door of his house. *A herpetologist.*

Must be a frog lover. That would be me!

That night, as he lay in bed, Jackson could hear the frogs. *Sure different from the city sounds, Jackson thoug*ht, tucking his hands under his head. It had taken Jackson a considerable time to get used to the difference between city and country sounds. Because of Dad's job, the family had moved from an apartment to the new housing development halfway across the country.

A line creased Jackson's forehead as he thought about the move. When Mom and Dad first broke the news, it was panic time. New school, new friends, new house. But their bribe of a bicycle–something he wasn't permitted in the city–slowly worked on the edge of his fears, nibbling away, as he imagined his new life.

A life that, in his mind, included a dog and a bike. *I might not be the most popular kid in school, but a dog will love me.* So far, the only pets he had were the frogs from the creek. Remembering how protective Mom had been in the city, he thought maybe he could use that as incentive. *A dog would protect me. Probably wouldn't work. Besides, Mom doesn't seem so uptight here. Well, I got the bike. Can't win them all.*

That reminded him about what Dr. T. had said. "Sentinels." Kind of like guardians. Not that frogs could ever take the place of a dog. *Frogs sure make a lot of noise. Crickets, too.* In the city he'd kept them in the refrigerator because of their noise. Here, even with the window shut, he could hear wild crickets and frogs down by the creek. Jackson chuckled quietly, thinking about bugs in the refrigerator. He shivered as he remembered. *They were quieter, but I was always afraid they'd get out and I'd end up taking a bite of food that crunched. Never thought I'd get used to these country noises, but now I'm kind of used to it.* Jackson yawned. He was anxious to talk more with his learned friend. *I'll go over right after school tomorrow. Right now, though, I think I'll just…*

Chapter 2

City to Country

"TIME to rise and shine!" Jackson's mom sang, rousing him from bed. He hurriedly brushed his teeth and washed up, then stood dressing in front of his big habitat. Last evening, he had placed the new frog into the terrarium in his room with several others he had caught. Spotted frogs. Most frogs have spots, but he knew the difference in this one: the light-colored stripe that runs along the upper lip.

As he dressed for school, Jackson watched his frogs. He noticed the new one hadn't moved from where he'd been placed the previous evening. *How odd*, he thought. Usually when he put a new frog into the aquarium, it immediately scrambled to a higher spot. This little guy hadn't moved at all.

"Hey, Newbie. I know, moving is scary. Don't worry, you'll get used to it. And you'll make friends." *Yeah, right.* Jackson thought back to his first pet frogs, bought from the pet store across the street from the apartment in the city. From the balcony, he could look down at the always congested, always noisy street. He could look across and see the corner grocery where Mom did the shopping. Directly across, there was a hotel with a large maroon canopy over the door. A friendly doorman in uniform often waved to Jackson when he noticed him up on the fifth floor. He knew Mom had a secret pact with Mr. Hayes to keep an eye on him. They thought they were so smart. Sneaky was what they were.

Speaking of sneaky, next to the hotel were several small shops, one of them, the Sneaky Snake Pet Store, was where Jackson bought his frogs and the crickets he fed them. There weren't many types of animals allowed in the apartment building, so he had no trouble choosing a pet. Mom would never have a snake. She confessed to knowing most snakes are not dangerous, but she was still a bit squeamish, so frogs were the default.

Funny how fearful she'd been about snakes in a pet shop, but Mom never thought about snakes around here. *Wonder if there are any in Dr. T's wild yard? Not gonna bring it up.*

As he dressed, Jackson thought back to his old life. His *good old life* he called it, though lately he wasn't so sure about that.

He remembered more than one time, lying in bed staring up at a cockroach on the ceiling and praying, *Don't fall on me. Don't fall on me.* He remembered craning his neck to keep an eye on the bug as he rolled up a newspaper and climbed up on the bed to try and swat it, usually unsuccessfully. Every time a new tenant moved into the building, the roaches would scamper to everyone else's apartment and they were always calling the exterminator. And every time, Mom invoked her old standby, "It'll be nicer when we move. And safer." Jackson never had an answer. He'd usually move to the balcony, where he'd look down at the vibrant city street. It was an exciting place to live. It was home, in spite of the occasional roach.

Mom interrupted his reverie, calling from the kitchen, "Breakfast is ready. Better get a move on or you'll miss the bus. Dad's left for work already." Jackson tied his sneakers and headed down the stairs.

Despite all his fears about moving, Jackson loved their new house. There were lots of interesting things in the neighborhood for a twelve-year-old boy to explore and he could ride his new bike without worrying too much about traffic.

Dad had promised they would visit a decrepit barn he could see across the fields. The old ranch was covered in high grasses now that the livestock was gone. Of course, there was the creek, his favorite place, and there were the frogs. And maybe snakes.

Jackson waited for the bus on the corner near the house and sat next to his friend, Raina. Her family had moved into the neighborhood over the Christmas break, so she didn't have a lot of friends, yet, either. School was too far to ride a bike, but there was plenty of time to ride after school and on weekends. Riding in the country (Mom and Dad called it the suburbs) sure was different from the city.

In the big city, the school was only about half a mile from home, but riding a bike wasn't a remote possibility. According to Mom, traffic was "a nightmare." Jackson and his neighbor Sawyer walked the distance together.

From the balcony, Jackson often watched the cars, buses and a flood of yellow taxis. Once, when he had the flu and stayed home from school, he discovered Flash and Dash, two older boys from his school, weaving in and out of the traffic. He'd seen a lot of adults on bikes: Cops, messengers for businesses, and the grown-up son and daughter of the Chinese family that owned the take-out place around the corner, but never kids.

If Sawyer was absent, Mom called a taxi. *Flash and Dash would probably think that was pretty funny.* He admired the boys. At school he learned of their renown and their well-deserved nicknames. Once, in the taxi on the way to school, Flash and Dash rushed passed the car. A chill ran down Jackson's back. *Flash and Dash. I wish I had a nickname. But you gotta earn a nickname and I don't even have a bike.*

By the time Jackson got on the bus, the only seat left was by Raina, as usual, as if everybody had planned it. *Figures. Guess the two nerdy new kids should sit together.* Jackson and Raina hadn't exactly hit it off when they first met. Jackson remembered how stuck up he thought

she was. She knew a lot of big words and Jackson wasn't sure ho
felt about that. *A girl who's smarter than me, but then, most everyone ..*

"Hey," he said to Raina, as they got off the bus in front of the
school. "Want to come over after school and see my frogs?" He wasn't
at all sure Raina would be interested in frogs. He wasn't really sure he
wanted to share his frogs with her, anyway. *Why did I say that?* She
was always carrying a book and she seemed to be interested in a lot
of things, but frogs? *She is a girl, after all. Well, if nothing else, she has
a bike. Maybe we'll go riding.*

"Sure! I love amphibians! Their name means 'two lives' because
they live on land and in water. I'll ask my mom if I can come over."

What a showoff, Jackson told himself. *Wish I could remember that
word Dr. T. called me last night,* Jackson thought. *Herbi. Nah, Herpi
something. I knew it last night! I bet* she *knows it.* "See you this afternoon," he said, as they entered the school and headed off in different
directions.

Chapter 3

A Wild Place

Raina kept her word and rode her bike over after school. Jackson saw her from his kitchen window. *She may be a girl, and she's pretty smart, but at least she doesn't treat me like a nerd, like some of the other kids at school.* Jackson ran out to meet her. "They're in my room," he said, trying not to seem too anxious. As they climbed the stairs, he explained, "I caught a couple this week. One just yesterday."

Entering the room, Raina peered into the terrarium. "Nice! Looks like they have everything they need. What do you feed them? Crickets?"

Jackson's eyebrows raised in surprise as he looked at her. "How'd you know that?"

"I raised frogs once when we lived in town. Of course, I didn't catch them myself, like you do. I had to buy their food at a pet store. The smaller ones didn't eat the crickets, though. Too big."

Jackson nodded.

"I collected bugs, like aphids, I found on the rose bushes in the apartment square." Raina peered into the terrarium. "He looks kinda dead."

"Yeah." Jackson removed the frog and placed it in his portable habitat. "Let's go show this to Dr. Thomson, my neighbor. He knows a lot about frogs. He knows a lot about everything. He's a little weird, but he's really nice."

Cutting through the opening in the low bushes that divided the yards, Raina stopped and gazed at Dr. Thomson's yard. "Wow."

"I know. Not your ordinary yard, but then, Dr. T. isn't your ordinary neighbor."

"There sure are a lot of flowers. Kind of wild, but pretty, in a strange way."

"Yep, wild. Dr. T. mostly plants natives. He says the kind of grass we all plant is exotic. Doesn't grow naturally here. He's always ranting about people watering and fertilizing. Poisoning our drinking water with…something."

Just then, Dr. Thomson emerged from behind a tall patch of shrubs. Raina jumped in surprise.

"A herpetologist AND a hydrologist! You're a budding scientist, Jackson." It was obvious he had overheard them.

Jackson swelled with pride. *Herpetologist. That's the word! Have to remember that.* "Hi, Dr. T.! This is my friend, Raina. She's a herpetologist, too. She likes frogs."

"Pleased to make your acquaintance, Raina. You know, herps are more than just frogs."

Jackson frowned. "What else is a herp?"

"There are the amphibians, of course."

"Toad and salamanders." added Raina.

"Yes, very good, young lady," said Dr. T., as he adjusted the small bucket hanging from his belt. "The cold-blooded reptiles, too."

Jackson jumped in before Raina could show him up again. "Snakes and lizards!" He knew what reptiles were.

"And crocodiles, turtles, tuataras…" she continued.

"Tuataras?" She surprised him again! Darn. It was especially important to Jackson that he not be shown up in front of Dr. Thomson. Especially by a girl.

"Well, you won't find any tuataras around here," answered Dr. T. "They're New Zealanders."

"I don't know, Dr. T.," Jackson said. "You never know what you might find in this nature preserve you've got here." Turning to Raina, he added, "I've seen all kinds of wildlife in this yard." He smiled to himself, remembering how squeamish Mom had been around the snakes in the pet store.

Shepherding them to the lawn chairs near the steps, Dr. T. said, "Yes, it's unfortunate all these houses were built in a riparian area. Say, how about some blueberries?"

Both faces lit up. "Sure!" Jackson answered, while Raina nodded her head vigorously. "Yes, please," she said.

Dr. T. passed them another small bucket he had sitting on the bottom step and they both helped themselves to a small handful. "Do these stain your teeth?" Raina asked.

"Oh, yeah. My mom made me swish something yucky around in my mouth for, like, ten minutes the last time I ate these."

"Probably peroxide," Dr. T. offered. "But maybe some other berries. Blueberries aren't too bad."

They were all quiet for a while, enjoying the berries. While he chewed, Jackson thought about their houses being built out here in the country. He was trying to remember what his neighbor had said just before the berries distracted him. He was no longer concerned about Raina showing him up "Dr. T., if you think it's so bad to build in a rip, a rip…"

"Riparian," Dr. Thomson helped him out.

"Riparian." The others waited while Jackson formed his words. "Your house is in the riparian area, too."

"Ah, how astute! Yes, it is. Have you noticed how different this house is from the others?" the doctor challenged the children.

You'd have to be blind not to notice, with all the wild plants surrounding it, Jackson thought. "Well, you have a front and back porch, and we all have patios."

"And you don't have grass," added Raina. "I like the wildflowers."

"Thank-you, my dear. This house was built over 125 years ago." They all turned to look at the old, two story house which stood out among the other, newer houses. "I was born in this house when it was still part of the ranch, before my family sold off most of the land. I know it's rare these days for people to be born in a house, much less live in it their entire lives."

"Did it make you sad to see the neighborhood where you grew up change so much?" Raina asked.

Dr. Thomson put his hands behind his head. "In some ways. But there has been good along with bad. There are now sewers to take away waste water from all the homes. When there were just a few old houses, like mine, we had septic tanks that dumped our waste water into the ground. So that's a good change.

"I've been very happy here, despite the changes. Got myself some good neighbors." He waved towards Jackson's house.

Jumping up from his chair, Jackson picked up the small habitat he had placed on the nearby picnic table. "Oh, Dr. T.! Remember the frog I caught last night?"

"How could I forget with my healthful acai concoction awakening my brain cells?" Looking towards the habitat, he said, "An admirable specimen."

Holding up the habitat for all to see, Jackson said, "Not so admirable today. He's dead."

Peering at the frog, Dr. T. said, "So I see. Was he healthy when you caught him?"

"I guess so. He was just sitting on a rock in the creek. He was a pretty easy catch. I noticed that he just sat and didn't climb up any branch when I put him in the bigger habitat."

"Ah, yes. Just perching. Lethargic."

Jackson had never heard the word before, but he had a pretty good idea what it meant. *Slow to move.* "That explains why he was so easy to catch." *And I thought I was so quick.*

"Maybe he was just old," suggested Raina.

"Could be. Not too many frogs die of old age. Most frog eggs are eaten. Tadpoles are, too. Those that reach adult stage are often dinner for predators, but many die from fungus. There's a really bad one ravaging frogs worldwide. Some actually do die from natural causes, that is, old age. That reminds me, and let me warn you, this is a completely unscientific question…"

Jackson smiled. He knew Dr. Thomson's tone meant he was up to something. He nudged Raina.

"Why did all the frogs croak after dinner?"

Jackson and Raina looked at each other, then back at Dr. Thomson.

"Because they ate poison flies."

Jackson grinned and Raina giggled.

Leaning on the back steps railing, Dr. Thomson spoke more seriously. "I'd be inclined to accept that many frogs die a natural death if I hadn't seen so many changes in the frog population along this creek and elsewhere."

"What kind of changes?" Raina asked.

"Let me show you." They started up the steps, but Dr. Thomson stopped with his hand on the doorknob. "Want to tell your mom first, that you're coming in?"

"We're good. I told her we were coming," Jackson said, as they stepped up.

Chapter 4

The Freaky Frogs

Dr. T. opened the back door and ushered them through the kitchen and into a series of rooms that were half library, half laboratory. *And I thought this house was weird on the outside.*

Jackson knew that Dr. Thomson was a professor of zoology at the university. But he hadn't realized there were so many animals in the house right next door. "Wow! Look, Raina, a real live alligator!"

"I'm not sure, but I think it's a crocodile."

Of course, Miss Know-it-all, Jackson thought, but didn't say.

"Crocodylus acutus. American crocodile." Said Dr. Thomson, walking up behind them.

"How can you tell the difference?" Jackson asked, bending to get a closer look through the aquarium glass.

Dr. Thomson waited for Raina to answer. When she didn't, he answered, "For one thing, the snout of a croc is longer and narrower. You can't see his teeth when his jaw is closed. Another is their habitat. Alligators live in fresh water, like the Florida Everglades and swamps. Many crocodiles can only be found in salt water but several crocs, including this guy, can be found in fresh water. He hasn't eaten in a couple of weeks. Doesn't need to. Want to feed him?"

"Oh, yes," said Jackson, while Raina made no reply. Jackson thought she must not be too crazy about the idea, but then she asked, "Well…What would we feed it?"

"I think I've got a few acai berries left."

"Uh uh," Jackson said, while Raina just wrinkled her nose.

"How about a fish?" asked Dr. Thomson, directing them to a tank across the room. "Raina, you catch one with this net, and Jackson, you can put it into the water in the croc tank. Keep your hands away. We don't want him to associate them with food."

"Sounds like a plan," Jackson said, as he watched Raina net a fish. She handed it off to Jackson. As soon as the fish hit the water, making a splash, the crocodile lunged, grabbed it, and swallowed it whole.

"Whoa! He was hungry."

"Yes. He'll grow to between 4 and 4.9 meters, about 13 to 16 feet, but he'll have to move before that."

"Where will you let him go?" Raina asked. "The creek's not salty."

Oh, so you don't know everything, Miss Smarty Pants," Jackson smirked. But he was beginning to admire Raina. *I guess even smart people don't know everything.*

Dr. Thomson answered Raina's question. "If the creek were salty, I wouldn't let him go. He's tropical and would surely die from the first cold winter. Besides, when you introduce exotic animals or plants into a new area many die, but when they have no natural enemies, some do take over, edging out native species."

At the word 'exotic', Jackson and Raina exchanged a quick glance, both thinking of Dr. Thomson's wild looking yard. *Wild, but not exotic,* Jackson remembered.

"You have a look around. See if you can find anything unusual. I have to make a phone call." Raina and Jackson thought the whole house, and their host, as well, were unusual, but they nodded, smiling gratefully. They moved from tank to tank, and stood, mesmerized, before the very large aquarium in the parlor.

"Ooh, look at that cool blue fish," said Jackson, pointing.

"It's a blue tang," Raina told him.

Of course she knows its name, Jackson thought. *Probably has a book about fish.* But he nodded, beginning to appreciate his knowledgeable friend, and he was glad to know the name of the beautiful fish. "My favorites are the clown fish."

"Mine, too!" Raina exclaimed. They looked at each other and smiled.

They wandered into the next room, where they stopped in their tracks, staring at several aquariums. "Unreal!" Raina said, staring at the unusual frogs.

Moving closer, they examined one tank, then another, their mouths open, occasionally uttering an "Oh, wow," or "Look at this one."

Doctor Thomson entered the room. "So, what do you think?"

"Awesome!" exclaimed Raina, and at the same time, Jackson said, "Freaky! Freaky frogs!" Then the questions tumbled out:

"Where did you get them? Why do they have so many legs?"

"Did they come from the creek?"

"Can they have babies?"

"How did they get this way?"

Doctor Thomson held up his hands. "Whoa! I know you have a lot of questions, but It's getting kind of late and I have a class. How about coming back tomorrow after school and we'll do some exploring in a riparian area."

"Cool," said Raina. At the same time Jackson exclaimed, "Awesome!"

* * *

Jackson yawned and put his arm over his eyes. He sat up in bed and yawned. Looking towards the terrarium, he said, "I better feed my own frogs before you go all Frankenstein on me, too." He was wondering for the hundredth time what could have caused Dr. T's frogs to become so deformed.

Jackson's dad was leaning against the doorpost of the bedroom as Jackson stood up and shuffled to the frog habitat. "Good morning!"

"Mmm," was all Jackson could muster.

"You were sure restless last night. Bad dreams?"

"Is it a nightmare if it really happened?" Jackson asked, as he dropped three crickets into the habitat.

Mr. McDowell laughed. "Was there a real monster under your bed?"

"No, but there are some real monsters in Dr. T's house."

His father had been at work until late the night before, so he hadn't heard about Dr. Thomson's frogs. Dad stood up straight, his brow wrinkled. "Oh?"

"Frogs. Freaky frogs."

"Freaky frogs? What are they, like, gigantic?" asked Dad.

"No, they're really weird. Some of them are missing a leg or two. Some have extra legs. One has a leg growing from behind its head."

"Wow. That *is* weird. So that's what you were dreaming about last night."

"I guess so."

"Did Dr. Thomson tell you what caused the deformities?" Dad asked.

"No, he had to teach a class. Said he'd explain it to us today."By this time, Jackson had dressed, and the two had reached the kitchen, where Mom was packing lunches. "Explain what to whom?" she asked. Then, "Better not dawdle with breakfast or you'll miss the bus." she said.

"Raina and I are going back to Dr. T's this afternoon to learn more about the frogs, if that's okay."

"Well…Maybe you should just stay outside. I'd like to know a little more about what Dr. T's got in there, first," Dad said.

Darn! He's going all protective, like Mom. Dad saw the look on his son's face and said, "We all want to know about this mystery, but just let Mom and me have a little chat with Dr. T., first. We want to be sure it's safe.

"Come on, get a move on, you two," Mom said. But Jackson had slowed down, thinking, *What if they don't let me go over to Dr. T.'s anymore?*

In the kitchen, Jackson gulped a glass of milk and peeled a banana. Dad scooped their lunches off the counter, and kissed Mom goodbye. "Don't kiss any frogs while we're gone. We might come home to find a wife and mother with three arms," he joked.

"I could get a lot more done if I had an extra arm," she answered. They all laughed as Jackson and Dad headed out the door. Jackson had joined in the laughter, but he had an uneasy feeling he couldn't quite understand. *Must be lack of sleep,* he thought.

Chapter 5

A Safari

JACKSON was standing at the kitchen sink eating a granola bar, trying to get a glimpse of Dr. Thomson out the window, when Raina came walking her bike around the corner of the house. He bolted out the door before she could reach the patio and park the bike. "Ready?" he asked.

"I ran into Kerry and some other kids I didn't know on my way over."

"I didn't know they lived in this neighborhood. They don't ride the same bus as us."

"They don't," Raina said. "Kerry's dad's a realtor, so he always knows when somebody new moves in. They just rove around looking for trouble."

"Did they give you any trouble?" Jackson asked.

"Well, they took me by surprise. Must have been hiding behind some bushes. They came out of a driveway and surrounded me. I was kind of scared for a minute, then they just took off. I don't think they meant me any harm, beyond a little scare. Which they accomplished."

"I've seen them ride by a couple of times." *And wished I had the nerve to go out and join them. Maybe not.* Jackson dismissed the thought. Come on, let's go see Dr. Thomson."

The Doctor was on the back porch, stuffing some things into a backpack, and called to them, "So, are you all ready for our little safari?"

Raina and Jackson stared up at him. "I didn't know we were going anywhere," said Raina.

"Oh, we won't go far." Dr. Thomson handed a portable habitat to Jackson and some nets to Raina. They began to walk through the maze of Dr. Thomson's yard, toward the creek.

"Hold up a minute." Dr. Thomson picked some leaves off a small plant and put it into his pail. "Oregano. For the sauce I'm making tomorrow."

Jackson and Raina exchanged a quick glance. "Smell it. Crumple it first," Dr. Thomson said as he offered them each a leaf. As they sniffed the leaves, Dr. Thomson said, "Let's really enjoy this trek. Use all of our senses."

Jackson stopped and sniffed. "Hey! There are a lot of different smells here." As they moved along, he asked, "Do you have a lot of spices planted here, Dr. T.?"

"A few herbs for cooking. I try to avoid exotics, remember. But oregano's great in homemade spaghetti sauce. I'm glad to see this survived the winter and is coming back. We're having an unusually warm year, a sign of changing climate." Before Jackson could ask about the other scents, Dr. Thomson stopped again, looking towards the creek. "Now close your eyes."

Raina and Jackson did as Dr. Thomson said. "Oh, I hear it! The creek!" cried Raina.

"It's so loud! How come it's so loud?" Jackson asked.

"It's no louder than before. You've just eliminated some of the distractions."

"Come on, let's go." Jackson started off, faster this time. Raina had to hurry to catch him. He was parting the brush to approach the creek, by the time Dr. Thomson got there.

"It's much cooler!" Raina said, rubbing her arms.

"It's a totally different environment. What do you see?"

"A boot," said Raina.

"A boot?" Jackson asked, looking in the direction Raina was pointing.

"Well, I'll be," said Dr. Thomson. He reached down to retrieve a boot which had wedged between a rock and the shoreline. He stretched to reach it and slipped on the wet, grassy incline. If he hadn't grabbed onto a thick grapevine, he would have slid into the water. He lay on his back, one hand stretched behind his head, clinging to the vine.

Raina and Jackson tried hard not to laugh but couldn't help themselves. They laughed even harder when Dr. Thomson said, softly, "That boot has given me more trouble than its worth. I'm seriously considering letting it drown."

"Is it yours, Dr. T.?"

"Yes, but now it's an only child. I thought I'd never see it again, so I cut up its mate to use the rubber for a drawer liner. Now my tools don't slide around when I open the drawer." Dr. Thomson stood, water dripping from his pants. Jackson said, "Here, Dr. T., let me get it."

"Okay. You hold onto my hand. I'll hold onto the vine. Let's take it slow."

Jackson reached the boot and grabbed it at the top. "Whoa, it's heavy!" Dr. Thomson took the water filled boot and turned it upside down, pouring it onto the grass.

"There's a fish!" The small fish wiggled in the grass, making it hard to catch. Raina picked it up by the tail, but it was so slippery, she lost her grip. Jackson got it, and cupping it in both hands, tossed it into the water. "Don't want to go down that slope."

"Guess that boot wasn't so useless, after all. I hope that fish wasn't like the old lady who lived in a shoe." He shook the boot.

The children looked up at him, puzzled looks on their faces.

"An old lady lived in a shoe?" asked Raina.

"She had so many children she didn't know what to do. The old nursery rhyme. Oh, never mind," said Dr. Thomson as he scraped a handful of mud out of the boot. "Now then, what do you see in this riparian environment?"

"Trees," answered Raina.

"Yes, there are trees here, though not all riparian areas have trees. They do all have some vegetation that doesn't grow elsewhere. Why do you think?"

"The water?"

"Most certainly! The riparian area helps filter out pollution and prevents erosion. It's a very happy little community. The water's good for the plants, which are good for the bugs, which are good for the fish and some fauna."

"Like frogs!" said Jackson.

"Like frogs," said Dr. Thomson, as he brushed a bug away from his face. "Hey, Raina, what did the frog say when he found a piece of paper?"

Raina shrugged and Jackson told her, "Ripit! Ripit!"

"You guys," Raina laughed, then asked, "If the riparian area's such a 'happy community,' then why are the frogs so messed up?"

"That, my dear, is the big question. Scientists and volunteers who love nature, are studying the issue all over the world."

"So, there are freaky frogs everywhere?"

"They're not everywhere, but frogs with extra limbs, or absence of limbs, and even digits, have been found in many places. The majority of states and Canada, too."

Raina leaned towards Jackson and whispered, "Digits are toes." Ordinarily he would have been embarrassed if an eleven-year-old girl had done that, but he was glad she had clarified. He wanted badly to understand all that Dr. T. was explaining.

"In California, some frogs that appear male, are laying viable eggs when exposed to common herbicides." Jackson looked at Raina, his nose scrunched up. "Viable?" he mouthed, but she was caught up in Dr. Thomson's commentary.

"Wow! That's weird." she said, and Jackson added, "Freaky!" It *was* pretty freaky if males were laying eggs. *Viable must mean the eggs are good and would hatch out live tadpoles.*

They walked along the stream without speaking and heard the splash, splash, splash of frogs jumping into the water. "Dr. T., is it true that 150 species have gone extinct?" Raina asked.

"A hundred and fifty?" Jackson's eyes were big.

"Easily that many in recent history, Dr. Thomson replied. About thirty percent of described frogs are threatened with extinction. But we are still describing many new species.

Well, we know there are frogs here. Let's slow down so we don't scare them," said Dr. Thomson, removing some berries from his pail, and throwing not two, but three, into the air, stopping to catch two of the three.

Jackson wondered if he had ever caught three and was about to ask when Dr. T. continued, "Frog species around the world are in trouble. More than half have gone extinct. Existing ones are suffering convulsions, and others, lethargic, just sitting."

There was that word again. Jackson could only guess what lethargic meant, but he knew it wasn't good. Then it hit him. "I wonder if my frog was already dying when I caught him?"

"The thought had occurred to me," said Dr. Thomson. He stood and handed a net to each of the children. "Are you ready to be surveyors?"

"Oh, yes!" Raina exclaimed. "Let's catch some!"

"Well, that would be fine, but our goal today is really just to scout this section of the creek to see if it's still accessible as a sentinel site."

"A sentinel site," Jackson said with pride. "Frogs are sentinels and give warnings of danger to humans. Like pollution in a river."

"Very good, Jackson. But this site will be for human researchers."

Raina was about to ask what kind of danger frogs would warn about, when Dr. Thomson cautioned, "Now, if you really do want to find some frogs, we'll have to be quiet. Let's walk single file, so we don't disturb too much underbrush. And we're only going to move a couple of meters at a time, scan, then move on, unless, of course, we find a frog."

Jackson pursed his lips. "Hmmm," he said. He knew from math class that a meter was only about three feet.

"It's gonna be hard to make myself stop and go like that," said Raina.

"That's what I was thinking," answered Jackson. He was itching to show off his frog catching skills in front of Raina.

Dr. Thomson, who was scanning ahead with a pair of binoculars, asked, "So, what's a frog's favorite restaurant?"

Thinking they were being tested, Jackson guessed, "A creek?" and Raina, "A riparian area?"

Without taking the binoculars from his face, Dr. Thomson answered, "Nope! I Hop." Before the kids could respond, he asked, "See that log on this side of the creek? About 15 meters ahead. There are a couple of leopards on it." The children hurried towards the log.

"Whoa! Remember, slowly. Otherwise, we'll scare them. They'll jump right off, into the water and we'll be up a creek without a frog." The kids grinned at each other. "Jackson, you go first. Sneak up behind the first one. Chances are, the other will jump, but there will be more."

Stealthily, Jackson approached the frog, and did, indeed, net it. As he took the frog to the habitat, Raina tried her luck, and also managed a catch. "This is so much fun!" she said. "I could do this all day."

"It sure would be cool to catch one with six legs," Jackson answered. "Wouldn't it?"

Chapter 6

Frog Surgery

WHILE they were catching the frogs, Dr. Thomson pulled out a clipboard and pen.

"What are you writing, Dr. T.?" Jackson asked.

"Data."

"Data?" the two asked in unison.

"Data. Facts. Information." The children noticed that Dr. T. had put on his polarized sunglasses and was looking into the water. "Our location, the date, the time, the condition of the water… Let's see, what else do you think would be important to note?"

After a moment Jackson volunteered, "The weather?"

"Weather. Good." Looking skyward, "What shall I say?"

"Clear and sunny," said Raina.

"If we had a thermometer, we could tell the temperature," said Jackson.

Nodding, Dr. T. handed him one he had clipped to his backpack. "So, what's the temp?"

Studying the thermometer so he wouldn't make any mistakes, Jackson reported, "27.7 degrees."

Peering over his shoulder, Raina said, "27.7? Are you sure?"

"Twenty-seven degrees sounds about right. That's Celsius, of course. That would be about 82 degrees Fahrenheit, as we measure in the U.S."

"I guess scientists use Celsius."

"Pretty much. Makes it easier to communicate and share information with scientists around the world." Dr. T. began writing again. "Jackson McDowell and Raina…"

"Salcedo," Raina answered.

"You're writing our names?"

"I'm writing our names. We're the surveyors." Dr. Thomson handed the clipboard to Raina and removed a tape measure and small box from the backpack. The children leaned in, watching, as he removed a frog from the habitat, laid it in one palm, and stretched it. Handing Jackson the small tape measure, he said, "Jackson, will you please measure from the frog's snout to this vent?" he asked, and pointed.

Jackson's hand shook slightly as he opened the tape measure. Looking up at Dr. Thomson's face for reassurance, he measured the length. "10.2 centimeters."

Dr. Thomson nodded. "Good. Raina, will you please write '10.2' centimeters for the frog's length? You can just write cm for centimeters."

Raina used her best handwriting. "How long is that in our language, Dr. T.?"

Dr. Thomson chuckled. "You think 'centimeters' is a foreign language, huh?"

Raina tilted her head to the side, grinning. "No, I just mean, how long is he in inches?"

"I know what you mean. I'm just giving you a hard time. How long does he look to you? From the tip of his snout to this opening," he said, pointing.

"Maybe four inches?"

"Right on!" said Dr. Thomson.

"Aren't we going to catch more frogs?" asked Jackson, rubbing his hands on his pants. "I want to catch one with more than four legs."

Dr. Thomson looked at Jackson a moment before answering, "Not really necessary. I just wanted to scout out the area. Some of my grad students are going to survey the area in a couple of months, when it's really warm. We're doing it every year for ten years. This is our seventh year."

"Ten years? Why?" Dr. Thomson had removed a small tool that looked like a knife

Before he could answer, Raina cried out, "What are you doing to the frog, Dr. T.? Are you going to cut off one of its legs?"

"Oh, my goodness, no!" Dr. Thomson had removed a small tool that looked like a knife. "I'm going to use this scalpel to make a small incision in the epidermis on the back of this little guy, just below his neck."

Jackson looked at Raina and mouthed, "Epidermis?"

"Skin," Raina whispered.

"Yes, skin. Good, Raina. You're quite the linguist."

Raina smiled and looked down at her feet. Jackson was both impressed and envious. It was a special honor to hear a compliment from Dr. Thomson. Jackson decided to let that one go, figuring it had something to do with Raina's big words. Instead, he asked," But why are you cutting the frog? Won't it hurt him?"

"Maybe just a little, but we'll put some antiseptic on the wound to help it heal. See this?" He was holding up a very small object he'd removed from the box. The children studied it.

"This is a passive integrated transponder, encased in glass. We call it a PIT or PIT tag. It's similar to what the vet inserts into pets." Dr. Thomson continued talking as he inserted the PIT into the frog and worked it down its back until it rested at the back of the frog's pelvis.

"We're not going to keep the frogs we capture. We'll insert PIT tags to track them. In fact, we're not going to capture any more frogs today. We'll leave that for the surveyors in July, when we'll likely find more adult frogs. That will give us a better indication of the population. I just wanted to give you a heads up so you'd know what to do during the actual survey. Which, by the way, will happen on four consecutive days."

"Four days in a row." Jackson was beaming, feeling pretty good that he hadn't had to ask about that one! Then it hit him. "So we'll know what to do? You're going to let us help?"

"Why not? You're available. You love nature. You're quite dexterous when it comes to catching frogs."

Jackson wiggled all his fingers. *Dexterous! Yep. I am good at catching frogs.*

Just then, Dr. Thomson clipped a piece of the frog's toe with a nail clipper.

"Ow!" Jackson said.

"More antiseptic," Raina said, handing the small bottle to Dr. Thomson.

"Thank-you, Dr. Salcedo," he said, handing the bottle back to her. "Would you do the honors?"

Raina dabbed the medicine onto the small, wounded toe. "But why did you do that, Dr. T.?"

Dr. T. was marking a small plastic bag into which he had put the clipping.

"Can you think of any reason?"

"To clone the frog?" asked Jackson.

"You guys have seen too many dinosaur movies. I think we have enough frogs in the world. At least around here. No, no cloning. The unique toe clip varies from year to year, so it's partly for ID purposes. Sometimes we do DNA studies, like in your Jurassic Park movies."

"Are you going to do a DNA study on this piece?"

"Probably not. But we'll add it to the collection. One clipping from one frog from one location is a very small sampling. Maybe later, when we capture more frogs." Dr. Thomson set the frog down, and it quickly hopped away. "Why don't you let his friend go, too, Jackson?"

Jackson released the second frog. "We'll be back to see you in a couple of months, little guy!"

Collecting their equipment, they headed back to the yard. "I'd invite you in, but I have another class tonight, so we'll talk more about the survey another time."

"Thank-you, Dr. T. This was so much fun!" said Raina.

"Yeah, thanks! It was **toad**ally awesome!"

"You're welcome! Thank YOU for your help! Oh, my boot! Let's see, where did that thing wander off to, now?"

Jackson and Raina hurried ahead and found the boot lying in the grass where Dr. T. had nearly fallen in. As Jackson reached for it, Raina grabbed his arm. "Look, a snake!"

A very small snake was poised near the boot until their sudden movement startled it. The snake slithered into the boot. Jackson and Raina looked at each other, then at Dr. Thomson, who was just catching up.

"I don't think you're gonna want to pick up that boot, Dr. T.," Jackson said. "There's a snake in it."

"I didn't get a good look at it. What did you see? Is it blotchy, striped or banded?"

"Well, it has long stripes," Raina said.

"Ah. A garter. Not poisonous." Dr. Thomson picked up the boot and turned it upside down. The snake moved quickly into the brush and out of sight. "I'm thinking if I just lay enough boots out here, I won't need a team to collect specimens."

"Are all your boots as good at catching wildlife as this one, Dr. T.?" Jackson joked. Raina elbowed him.

Dr. Thomson laughed and asked, "Why couldn't the snake talk?"

"Does it have something to do with the boot?" Raina asked, just as it dawned on Jackson.

"He had a frog in his throat!"

"Ohhhh," groaned Raina. "Shoulda seen that one coming."

"I think it will be great having you with the team this year," Dr. Thomson told them. "You're very observant. I'm really looking forward to seeing what effect the change from farmland to housing development is having on the waterway: positive or negative? Our frog friends are a good indication." Opening his hands, palms up, he added, "That's why we call them an indicator species."

"See you guys on Sunday, if you're around. I'm going to a conference tomorrow and I won't be back in town until Saturday evening." Dr. T. waved and headed to his back door, while Raina and Jackson turned towards home.

Both kids were quiet, deep in their own thoughts. *An indicator species,* thought Jackson. *One more mystery.* His thoughts were interrupted by Raina. "What does the housing development have to do with the creek?"

"Well, I guess there are no more cows drinking from it. This used to be a cattle ranch." The two walked on in silence. "Want to come in?"

"No, I'd better get home. I have to study for a test coming up on Friday. See you on the bus tomorrow."

"Yep. Good luck on your test," Jackson called as he headed to the door.

Chapter 7

An Interesting Question

A T the dinner table Jackson's dad asked, "So, did you find any five-legged frogs on your adventure?"

"No, but you won't believe what Dr. T. did to a frog!" Both Mom and Dad stopped eating and stared at Jackson.

"I thought Dr. Thomson was good to the wild animals. He didn't hurt it, did he?" asked Mom.

"Well, the frog would say yes. He put some kind of tracker in the frog's back. A transponder, I think it's called. But the frog seemed to be okay when we let him go." Jackson told his parents about the survey. "I just can't wait until July when the real survey happens. Dr. T. said Raina and I can help!"

Mom and Dad looked at each other. "Really? It does sound like he's taught you what to do," said Mom.

"Do you think you could do surgery on a frog?" asked Dad.

"Not sure. But I don't think I'll be doing that."

"Not until you get to biology in high school, anyway," Dad said. "At least not 'till tenth grade when you cut up frogs in biology class."

Jackson's eyes opened wide. "Really? They make you cut up frogs in biology? Why? There won't be any frogs left if every kid does that!"

"Oh, they'll be frogs that were raised in a lab," Mom told him.

"Actually, I think in a lot of places, they're dissecting frogs digitally," Dad added.

"Dad was telling me about Dr. Thomson's frogs," said Mom. "Jackson, I don't want you going into his house, until we've had a chance to talk to him about what made them that way. I don't want you exposed to anything dangerous."

Jackson's face fell. "Yes, Ma'am. Dad already told me." Jackson answered, but thought, *Don't they know Dr. T. is my friend and would never let me get hurt?*

The conversation moved on to the day's other events. After helping clear the dinner dishes, Jackson started for the den to study for Friday's test and complete his homework, but Dad called to him, "Jackson, wanna hear a frog joke?"

"You know a frog joke?" Jackson was surprised. He expected frog jokes from Dr. T., but Dad?

"Well, it's not too original. When you take biology, you'll probably hear it. But you can be the first to tell it to your class."

Jackson stood, expectantly, and Dad said, "Once upon a time..." Jackson rolled his eyes, and Mom and Dad laughed.

"Okay, okay, I guess you're too sophisticated now for 'once upon a time.' How about this?" Dad continued, "A frog was bored, so he decided to go visit a fortune teller. The lady took his flipper in her hand and traced a line with her index finger. 'You have a very short life line, but I can tell you this: Next month you will meet a beautiful young woman.' 'Cool. Where?' asked the frog. 'In her biology class.'"

Jackson looked puzzled at first, then pursed his lips and shook his head, which made Mom and Dad laugh again "I know, I know. Not as good as Dr. T's jokes," Dad said.

"Oh, I think he'll like it. I'll definitely tell him."

"Don't mention my name!" Dad called to Jackson, who was already in the den. He sat down at his desk, but his mind was on the survey

and he found it difficult to concentrate. *Now, if the test were on frogs*
…

* * *

Thursday seemed to pass quickly, at least science class. Jackson told
them about the survey.

"There's no such thing as a six-legged frog," said CK, who was
always cracking jokes. Before Jackson or Mr. Dorr could respond,
CK, the class cut-up, got out of his seat in the front row, bent down,
and hopped like a frog. "Ribbit, ribbit."

After hopping, he moved his legs forward a second time, and fell
onto his side. "The middle legs would get in the way of the back legs!"
He shouted to be heard, since he had thrown the entire class into a
fit of laughter and exclamations.

Allowing the class to enjoy the moment, Mr. Dorr eventually re-
gained order and asked, "What do the rest of you think? Would extra
legs, or lack of legs cause a frog any problems?"

"He sure wouldn't be the best dancer at the prom!" blurted CK,
causing a second round of chatter.

Morgan, a quiet girl in the back of the room raised her hand. "Yes,
Morgan?" Jackson
leaned towards her, not wanting to miss a word.

"Would he be able to catch food?" she asked.

CK again rose from his seat, darting his head from side to side and
sticking his tongue in and out rapidly.

"Morgan?" asked Mr. Dorr, He gave a look to CK that said, 'Sit
down," which CK did.

"I understand a frog captures prey with its tongue, but would it be
able to move into place to catch, say, a fly?"

"Good question. A frog's mobility, or lack thereof, might hinder its
ability to feed itself. Speaking of moving into place, what else would
it be difficult for a frog to do?"

Two hands went up. "Jeannine?"

"Swim?"

"And why would that be a problem?" The class was quiet.

"What might he be swimming towards or away from?" asked Mr. Dorr.

Several hands went up, including CK's. Eyebrows raised, Mr. Dorr called on CK.

In the deepest voice he could muster, CK said, "The monster from the deep lagoon." The laughter was so loud this time, it nearly drowned out the bell. Above the din, Mr. Dorr called out, "Tonight, instead of the homework I was planning on assigning, think about what else a lack or surplus of legs or digits could make it difficult for a frog to do. Something besides capturing food that might affect the frog population. See you tomorrow!"

* * *

Jackson reached the bus at the same time as Raina. "Jackson," she asked, as they boarded, "What happens if a frog's parking meter expires?"

Jackson shook his head.

"He gets toad."

"Good one! You have to tell that to Dr. T. Oh, I told my science class about Dr. T's frogs and now I have frog homework!"

"Cool!"

Stowing his backpack, Jackson asked, "Raina, what do you think a frog couldn't do if it didn't have all its legs, or digits?" Jackson was feeling pretty good about using the word 'digits', instead of 'toes'. *I'll catch up to her if I hang around Dr. T. long enough,* he thought.

"Is this a joke?" Raina asked.

"No. We were talking about the freaky frogs and Mr. Dorr told us to think about it for homework."

Hmmm…If a frog were missing a leg or toes…Swim? I know I'd have trouble!"

Just then, Miranda, who was in Jackson's science class, bounced past and plopped into the seat directly behind them. Miranda was about the bounciest person Jackson knew. She always seemed to be dancing or singing, as though she had an invisible iPod. The bus started up and was noisy, with many conversations going on at once. Miranda rested her hand on the back of their seat and leaned forward to speak. "I've been thinking about that all afternoon. Remember it has to be something that would affect the population."

The idea seemed to occur to them all at the same time. "Mate?" asked Raina.

"Mate!" Jackson and Miranda blurted at the same time.

"Checkmate!" came from somewhere in the back of the bus, no doubt from Barry, the kid who was always coming up with jokes on the spot. Sometimes his exuberance got him in trouble with the bus driver. The three friends all laughed. "I guess we were a little loud," said Miranda, starting to bounce from side to side, obviously 'hearing' a song they couldn't.

"We aren't any louder than everyone else on this bus." Jackson said. "I'm not so sure about that. Mating, I mean. Swimming, I can see, but mating? We'll have to ask Dr. T. when we see him," Jackson said. "I'm going to do some research when I get home."

"Google 'frog abnormalities,'" Raina suggested.

Abnormalities. Leave it to Raina, he thought, but he was no longer feeling resentment towards her. *Her frog jokes are as good as mine and Dr. T's. H*e reached for his backpack and waved good-bye to his friends. "See you tomorrow."

Chapter 8

It's Just Biology

O N Friday, Jackson could hardly wait for Raina's stop. He wanted to discuss what he'd learned with her, before talking about it in class. When she got on, Jackson thought she was trying unsuccessfully to repress a smile.

"What are you so happy about this morning?" he asked. "I thought you had a test today."

"Oh, I do, but I was thinking about what I learned last night. About frogs."

"You researched it, too?"

"Uh-huh," Raina answered. "Very interesting."

Jackson was actually a little embarrassed to be discussing the subject with a girl, and was glad Miranda was sitting so far from them. It was bad enough to be talking about sex with a girl, but two girls?" *It's not sex, goof ball. It's biology.* "Yes, interesting. Did you find that they have trouble mating if they're missing a foot or a digit or two?"

"Uh-huh." I guess it's harder for the male to get into the correct position and hold on to the female." Raina was quieter than usual.

Jackson was thinking maybe she was a little embarrassed, too. *Think like a scientist,* he reminded himself. *I can't wait to have this conversation in class,* he thought. "Well, I guess that would affect the population."

"For sure."

Yep. She's embarrassed. Like me. "Hey, Raina! What has more lives than a cat?"

Raina grinned. "Has to be frogs."

"Yep! They croak every night!" They both laughed and Jackson said, "I'll let you know what else we come up with in class."

"I can't wait! See you later," Raina said.

"See ya." Jackson answered. "Good luck on your test."

* * *

When Jackson sat down behind him, CK was showing something he had in his pocket to his neighbor. He couldn't be sure, but it looked like a frog. *I've got frog on the brain,* he said to himself.

Mr. Dorr picked up a marker and walked to the board. "Our discussion yesterday began with frog abnormalities—freaky frogs." At the word 'abnormalities,' Jackson thought of his and Raina's talk.

Mr. Dorr continued, "There are some big problems in frog populations around the world, with some species disappearing completely. Let's hear what you've come up with regarding problems a frog might have if he were missing, or had limbs or digits in the wrong place."

"Frogs have gone digital?" The class didn't respond to CK's shenanigans this time. They were all interested in the topic and several hands were already in the air.

"Since Jackson initiated this discussion, let's let him go first."

Jackson's face flushed, but mindful of his pride, he said, "Well, like Morgan and Jeannine said yesterday, they might have more trouble catching prey, so they couldn't feed themselves properly."

"That would ultimately affect the population. Anything else?" Mr. Dorr asked.

"Escaping from predators," Jackson said.

"What about it?"

Jackson answered, "They couldn't swim as well, so it would be harder to escape."

"Good review, Jackson." Mr. Dorr turned to write on the white board.

Jackson was sure now. The thing in CK's pocket was a frog. He watched, as CK removed the frog and lowered it to the floor. He tried to look at the frog without being obvious, to see if it would move. It did.

Mr. Dorr asked, "Anybody find other problems a malformed frog might have, keeping in mind, a problem that could affect the population?"

Jackson knew he had thought of a major problem, but was reluctant to volunteer the information, which was fine, since there were many hands raised. *Give someone else a chance*, he thought.

"Brian?"

Brian always had a good answer. "They could have problems mating." Jackson relaxed, sliding lower in his seat, relieved someone else had brought up the subject. *Nobody ever thinks Brian's a nerd. Just smart.*

"How so?" asked Mr. Dorr.

"They don't even need to be missing a whole leg. If they're missing two specific digits, the males can have trouble holding onto the female."

A murmur of voices arose from across the room. Brian's hand was raised again, and he turned to look at those behind and around him. He obviously had more to say.

"Go, on, Brian," Mr. Dorr said, but he was looking across the room, where the voices were coming from.

"Amphibians live on both land and in water, they can absorb a lot of chemicals that run off nearby surfaces, which messes up a lot of stuff like digestion, urination, mating. Some frogs are being found with both male and female organs."

"A boy-girl combo. A birl," said CK.

"So, you've just summed up several problems in one sentence," Mr. Dorr said, ignoring CK.

One very long sentence, thought Jackson. He really admired Brian. *No wonder the kids call him Brian the Brain. I'lll never have a nickname like that.*

Mr. Dorr continued, "If you can't digest your food properly, if you can't urinate and rid your body of waste, if you can't mate…" He held both hands out, palms up. "Not much hope for your survival."

CK interrupted, singing "Dum da dum dum," raising a few giggles.

"Dum da dum dum, indeed. You have more, Brian?" he asked.

"There are other deformities, too: missing eyes, and tails that weren't absorbed when the tadpoles were becoming frogs. Missing legs, not just extra ones."

Mr. Dorr nodded. "So, if frog populations are stressed, and the health of frogs indicates the health of the environment, what does that mean for the environment?"

Caught up in the discussion, several responses came at the same time:

From Denise, "Bad news!"

Trish said, "It's stressed, too."

Grinning at each other, CK and his neighbor sang in unison, "Dum da dum dum."

Mr. Dorr continued. "That's why Jackson's team is surveying, looking for sentinels. Frog warnings."

Jackson's team. It's really Dr. Thomson's team. But it was cool to hear Mr. Dorr say 'Jackson's team,' as though he really were a herpetologist. *Not having any more trouble remembering that one!*

"So, anyone come up with some possible causes for what we're seeing in frog populations?"

Mr. Dorr called on the girl whose hand shot up first among many.

"Changes in climate."

"Oh, not the global warming thing." from a voice in the back.

Turning to look at her classmate, the girl said, "Polar ice caps are melting. Plant and animal species are moving further north..."

Before she could finish, a ruckus broke out on the other side of the room. "Eek!" squealed one girl. A boy sat on top of his desk, and Miranda actually stood on hers.

Several students got up and converged near the doorway, just as it opened and closed behind a boy with a small pack of papers for Mr. Dorr. The boy, eyes wide, took a step back, glancing from the crowd of students surrounding him, to the teacher.

"Just set them on my desk, please," Mr. Dorr told the boy, heading towards the clump of students and parting them, as he approached the object of their attention. Denise reopened the door and stooped, retrieving a very flat frog which had been caught between the door and door jamb. She held it up by one foot, handing it off to Mr. Dorr. The frog had tried to escape when the boy opened the door and got caught when it closed.

"Yay, Denise to the rescue!" someone said. *That's the truth,* Jackson thought. *I'm good at catching live frogs, but a freshly smooshed, dead one? Bleah!*

"Everybody back to your seat, please. I think we're safe from the invasion of the frogs." Excited voices lowered, as order returned. Laying the frog on his desk, Mr. Dorr looked at Jackson. "Unless there are more. There aren't, are there?"

"No Sir," Jackson stammered. "Uh, I mean, I don't know, Sir. I mean, I didn't bring it. Sir."

Mr. Door turned to CK, and all eyes followed his gaze. "We need to channel that enthusiasm, CK. Please remain seated when the bell rings."

A couple of students said "Ooooh!" Still grinning, CK lowered his head, and answered, Yes, Sir.

"All right, everybody. We've heard some good points about the effects of the changing climate, which are well documented, but that's a whole other topic. Right now, anyone else have a theory on why frogs are turning up with extra or missing limbs?" the teacher asked.

Just then, the bell rang, but Mr. Dorr held his hand up to stop the students who were rising from their seats. "I want to pose a question for you to think about over the weekend. Would there be more harmful contaminants in a ditch by a supermarket parking lot, or in a creek on a farm?

"Have a great weekend, everybody. No homework, but if anybody wants to do some further research on freaky frogs…" The rest of his sentence was drowned out as the class, except for CK, rose to leave, chattering as they went, many calling "Good-bye, Mr. Dorr."

Chapter 9

An Old Ranch

JACKSON was happy it was Saturday, even though he wouldn't be able to discuss frogs with any of his frog friends, as he was coming to think of them. Dr. Thomson was still at his conference and Raina was going shopping and to a movie with her mom.

But Dad had promised they would check out the old barn across the field and Dad always kept his promises. It would be great to explore, but better yet, it would be great to explore with Dad.

Saturday breakfasts were always fun and delicious. No one had to rush to get to work or school, so they cooked a big meal. Jackson's favorite was pancakes, especially when Dad let him put in chocolate chips or nuts. Everyone helped. Mom cut up fruit, Jackson set the table, and Dad cooked. After the blessing, Dad asked, "So, what are you planning to do with yourself today? Catch more frogs?"

Jackson's face dropped. *How could he forget? I've been looking forward to this all week.*

Dad reached over and gave a little shove to Jackson's shoulder. "You thought I forgot our mission, didn't you?"

Jackson smiled, relief all over his face.

"How could I forget? I've been looking forward to this all week."

"Me, too!" said Jackson. "What do you think is in that old barn?"

"I wonder. Maybe some old farm equipment?"

"Or tack," Mom suggested.

"Tack? What's that?"

"Oh, stuff horse riders use. Bridles, saddles, rope, stirrups, halters." Jackson's mom used to ride at summer camp when she was a teenager.

"They cleared that place out pretty fast. Remember when we were first looking for a house and we rode out this way? This development wasn't even started."

"There were just cows. Lots and lots of cows," said Mom. "So there had to be a lot of cowboys. Nowadays cowboys use pickup trucks, too, but I think that ranch was there a long time. Back then, they just used horses. Hence, the tack."

"Yep, it would probably be easy to forget something hanging on a nail, if you're clearing out fast," added Dad.

"Why do you think they left so fast?" Jackson asked.

"Dunno. Maybe the developer who bought the land forced them to. Speaking of fast, the faster we help clean up, the faster we can mosey on over and check out that barn, Pardner."

"I'm on it," Jackson said, as he stood and gathered plates and cups to carry to the sink.

* * *

Crossing the fields, heading for the barn, Jackson asked, "So this was a cow pasture?"

"Yep. Better watch where you step!"

"Oh, gee!" Jackson looked down, checking the bottom of first one, then the other shoe. "How many cows were here?" Looking at Dad, he realized he was being kidded again. Jackson side bumped his father. "Dad!"

"What?"

They walked for a while and Jackson stopped. "A farm's supposed to be a healthy place, isn't it?"

"What makes you think so?" asked Dad.

"Oh, you know, wide open spaces and all. That was Mom and your big selling point when you first told me about the move."

Dad laughed. "Yeah, I guess fresh air is good for anybody. But there's more to a farm than fresh air. Why do you ask?"

Jackson tried to remember how Mr. Dorr had phrased the home-work question. "Do you think it would be healthier for a frog to live in a ditch beside a supermarket parking lot or in a culvert on a farm?"

Dad looked at his son. "What an interesting question. Where'd that come from?"

They began walking again. Jackson told Dad about the class discussions, the research he and his classmates were doing on the different frog abnormalities and their causes.

"Is this related to Dr. Thomson's surveys?"

"Kind of. Well, yeah, I guess so. We were studying oceans, but when I told them about the frog survey, Mr. Dorr kind of went with it. He's pretty cool that way."

"Yes, he's a good teacher."

"Hey, Dad, how can you tell if a frog has no ears?"

"Dr. Thomson's frogs have no ears?" Dad asked.

"No, it's a joke."

"Oh, sorry. Let me think. How do you know if a frog has no ears? I give up."

"You yell 'Free flies' and he doesn't come."

Dad shook his head, smiling.

By this time, they were at the barn. The big doors were barred, but there was a smaller doorway on the side that had no door on it. When they entered, they realized the larger doors on the back end of the barn were off as well, and there were a lot of shingles missing from the roof, so there was ample light inside.

"Guess we didn't need flashlights," Jackson said. "Gross! What is that stuff?"

A black puddle had leaked from one of the rusty barrels stacked in the barn. Dad stooped down to get a closer look. "It's oil."

"Oil? What for?"

"Oh, I'd guess equipment. Trucks, tractors."

"Tractors? I thought this was a ranch, not a farm."

"They probably grew feed for the cattle. That would be the most economical way to feed them. Grow your own."

"Oh, yeah." They walked around the barn for a few minutes, peeking into stalls. "Wow! What's this?"

They had arrived at a large wooden structure, about thirty feet tall. "That confirms it," said Dad. "This is a hay baler. You've seen bales of hay. It makes it easier to stack the hay. Some ranchers who grow more hay than they need themselves, sell it, and baling the hay makes it easier to transport."

Jackson walked around the baler. "There would be oil from cars in the ditch by the supermarket. Which wouldn't be good for the frogs. But there might be oil in the farm culvert, too." He sat down on the edge of a trough and Dad joined him.

"Well, there could be. But I think the pollutants that come off a ranch aren't primarily oil and gasoline," answered Dad.

"What are they?"

"Okay, let's think this out. If they raise a crop, what does it need?"

"Oh, yeah, the fertilizer! We talked about that in class."

"But that's not all."

Jackson thought. *What else on a farm could hurt us? What else are the frog sentinels warning us about?*

"If you have a lot of cows, what else are you going to have a lot of?" Dad asked.

"Hamburger!" They both laughed.

"Well, that's a good thing, unless you're a vegetarian. Or a cow." Dad paused. "Remember what I joked about when we were crossing the field?"

Jackson's head snapped up. "Cow poop?"

"Cow poop. I think cowboys would call them cow pies."

"Oh, yummy." They laughed again.

"Even with good things, too much can be bad. I'm sure there was a lot of runoff into the creek." Jackson mulled that over.

"Gettin' kind of warm out here," Dad said. "Seen enough?"

"I guess. But I really don't want to go home yet."

Dad, put an arm around Jackson's shoulder. "Me, neither. It's great to spend time with my best bud." Jackson smiled.

"Say, why don't you teach me how to catch a frog," Dad said.

"Really?"

Putting his arm around Jackson's shoulder, Dad said, "Maybe we can catch one of those six-legged hoppers."

Jackson had been thinking the same thing. "Well, I'd kind of like to. But then, I'd kind of like not to."

Chapter 10

A Big Hole

"Our first picnic of the year. Great idea. I'll set up the umbrella," Dad said. "Jackson, you go wipe off the table, while I dig up a tray to carry the food outside."

After cleaning the table, Jackson helped Mom carry the lunch out. They were surprised to see Dad and Dr. Thomson talking on the patio.

"How are you, Ron?" Mom asked.

Dr. Thomson rose to give Mom a hug. "Great, Lorraine. Thanks. How's our budding herpetologist?" he asked, tapping Jackson on the shoulder.

Jackson blushed and asked, "Can Dr. T. stay for lunch, Mom?"

"It's a done deal," Dad answered." Sorry I didn't give you a heads-up, Hon," he said to Mom.

"No problem. There's plenty. I'll just get another place setting."

When Mom returned, Dad asked Jackson to say the blessing. "All things bright and beautiful. All things green and small. All things wise and wonderful, the Lord God made them all. Thank you, Lord. Amen."

The grownups echoed, "Amen."

Dad looked at Jackson as he picked up the bread. "Green and small, huh?" Jackson grinned.

"Mmm. This looks delicious." Dr. Thomson took a bite of fried chicken. He looked at Jackson and said, "One day a baby frog asked his mother, 'Mommy, who's smarter, chickens or frogs?' 'Frogs are, dear,' answered the mother frog. 'How do you know?' asked the baby. Mother answered, 'Have you ever seen Kentucky fried frog?'"

Jackson was still chuckling when Dr. Thomson addressed the grownups. "You're gonna' get a lot of use out of this umbrella this year. Seems like it warms up earlier every year."

"Isn't that the truth," Dad answered.

"And every summer seems hotter than the one before. Or maybe the older I get, the more I feel the heat," Mom added.

"Just be sure to protect yourself. An umbrella's a good start."

"Oh, Mom's always slathering lotion on us in the summer."

"That's good. Protect your eyes, too," Dr. Thomson said, looking directly at Jackson.

"My eyes?"

"Your eyes. From the UV rays."

"We should probably invest in some sun glasses for you. For all of us," Mom said.

"Do you know what UV rays are?" Dad asked Jackson.

"Not really. I just know they're not good."

"That's true. That's why we wear UV rated sunglasses to protect our eyes and sunscreen to protect our skin."

"What did the cavemen do? Stay in their caves during the day and only come out at night? I know they didn't have sunglasses."

"No, they didn't," answered Dr. Thomson. "But they didn't have holes in the ozone, either."

"Holes in the what?" Jackson managed to mumble, with a mouthful of potato salad.

Mom tilted her head, frowning, then turned to hear Dr. Thomson's answer.

"Ozone. It's a natural gas. There's a layer of it in the Earth's atmosphere that absorbs most of the sun's ultraviolet light. Thirty years ago, the hole over the Antarctic was a huge sensation. Now it's shrinking and the hope is, it'll be completely healed by 2050."

"Then, holes in the ozone layer are bad," Jackson said.

"Oh, yes." Doctor Thomson had unhooked his pail from his belt and was offering berries all around.

Jackson hoped Dr. T. would toss some up and show Mom and Dad his unusual talent, but asked, "I don't get it, Dr. T. What made the holes?"

As if he had read Jackson's mind, Dr. T. had turned sideways in his chair and tossed two berries into the air, catching them without standing.

"Whoa!" said Dad.

"Watch me, Dad," Jackson said, tossing a berry up. It hit the underside of the umbrella and landed in the potato salad. Jackson used a spoon to retrieve it from the bowl. Standing, a sheepish grin on his face, he began collecting dishes. "I'll just take some of this stuff inside."

"Wait a minute. I have an idea. Let's all stand up, away from the table and see who can catch the most berries," Dad suggested.

"Not me! You guys go ahead. I'll clean up," said Mom, stacking dishes onto the tray.

Jackson and Dad had several misses before Dr. Thomson told them, "Start with your arm low. Release the berry when your arm is about here. Don't flick your wrist. That changes the trajectory. You want it to go straight up."

Jackson's next try was a miss, but the next one went straight up, then down, and right into his mouth. Dad and Jackson high fived and Dr. Thomson nodded. "You're a quick study, Jackson."

Dad and Dr. Thomson sat down again, while Jackson continued to throw berries into the air, catching one every once in a while. When he finally sat, he asked, "Dad, did you talk to Dr. T. about–you know. The frogs at his house?"

"I did. Funny thing. Or maybe not so funny. Those frogs are having the same problem we people are having. Thin ozone."

"No kidding. So UV light is making freaky frogs?

"Looks that way," Dr. Thomson answered. "Indirectly, anyway."

"What's making the holes in the ozone?" asked Jackson.

"Hmmm. Tough one. Simple answer? Greenhouse gasses."

Jackson immediately thought about the green house in Mr. Wilmoth's yard, just east of them. Dad and Dr. Thomson saw him looking in that direction and followed his gaze.

"Mr. Wilmoth's greenhouse is a perfect example. Have you ever been inside it?"

"Just once. He called me over to give me some herbs he'd grown. They were awful, by the way, just in case he offers you any." Then he remembered Dr. T. was always collecting, and eating stuff from his own garden, and was sorry he had said it.

"How did it feel in the greenhouse?" Dr. Thomson asked.

"Kind of warm. Nice." Jackson was thinking and the grownups waited. "It kind of reminded me of the car, when it's parked on the street on a sunny day. In the wintertime, that is. In the summer, it's wicked hot in a parked car."

"Exactly!" Dr. Thomson said. "The glass walls and roof traps energy and heat from the sun. Keeps it from getting out. So, it gets warmer and warmer during daylight, and even keeps the air and plants warm at night."

"Cool! No, I mean, hot. What's that got to do with the ozone?"

"Well, the Earth is like a greenhouse. Sunlight comes through our atmosphere and warms us, then is reflected back into space. But more and more greenhouse gases trap more and more heat, making the Earth warmer and warmer. These gases are also ozone eaters. They're eating holes in the ozone, which lets in more…"

"UV light! I get it!"

"We are doing better. Back in 1987 we stopped using an accelerant in our refrigerators and spray cans like hair spray and shaving cream. The ozone hole is getting smaller but it's still a big problem. Some of my students are working on a project right now with frogs and UV light."

"What does UV light have to do with frogs?" Jackson asked, his head tilted, as he pondered the frogs.

"What SPF sunscreen do you think frogs wear when they sun themselves?" Dad asked.

"Oh, no! Dr. T., do you think UV light is making the frogs lose their legs?"

"I can pretty much guarantee it, from experiments in the lab. You know, of course, their legs don't just fall off. They're being born without them, or with extras, and with other abnormalities."

"We have to stop it! Those poor frogs!" Jackson jumped up from his seat. "You don't think people will start being born with extra legs, too, do you, Dr. T.?"

"No, no, no. That's not going to happen. But skin cancer and eye problems are a very real consequence of ozone holes. There is hope, Jackson. We've learned a lot about those harmful refrigerants – in the cans and refrigerators and we're still learning."

Dad stood, too, saying, "Jackson, give Dr. Thomson a break. We're going to move some lumber from his truck to the garage. Want to help?"

"No thanks. I've got something I want to do inside. See you later," he said with a little wave, as he headed for the computer. He didn't notice Dad and Dr. Thomson staring after him, as he muttered, "UV light. Frog abnormalities."

Chapter 11

The Rappers

Monday morning brought rain and a return to cooler temperatures. Raina was all smiles when Jackson boarded the bus and found a seat in the row across from her. "Nice frog weather, huh?"

"I'll say. If the UV rays don't get them."

"Huh? What are you talking about?" Raina asked.

"UV rays." Jackson told her what he had learned. "Did you know you can still get a sunburn when it's cloudy?"

"Nuh-uh!"

"Uh-huh. UV rays." Jackson told her everything he had learned over the weekend. He had so much to tell, he forgot to ask about her weekend in town, but Raina was all ears and didn't seem to mind. "I can't wait to tell Mr. Dorr what I found out."

Raina rose to get off the bus. "Well, you'll get to soon enough. See you later."

"Later!" Jackson answered.

* * *

Jackson felt pretty excited, looking forward to telling what he'd learned. He took his seat behind CK who, he noticed, was in rare form. CK was hunkered down in his seat with his arms crossed. He was wearing a leather jacket. *Why not?* Jackson thought. *It is cooler today than it has been lately.* What was unusual, though, was CK wearing a pair of big, dark sunglasses. *Weird for a day like today.*

Mr. Dorr picked up a marker from the desk and headed for the whiteboard. "Hope everyone had a great weekend," he said, as he wrote

POSSIBLE CAUSES OF
FROG ABNORMALITIES:

"There's something we haven't mentioned and that surprises me. Jackson said his neighborhood is built on an old ranch, near a creek. Think about what that means for all wildlife, not just frogs."

"No more home, home on the range for those cows." said CK.

"Exactly. Habitat loss," Mr. Dorr wrote as he spoke. "So far, we have, one, habitat loss; two, climate change. Which is causing a lot of drought." He continued writing. "Three, chemical runoff."

Jackson's hand shot up. He had an answer for number four: UV light, but he was disappointed when, turning to the class, Mr. Dorr asked, "What about these chemicals? What are they? Miguel?"

Miguel answered, "Pollution."

"Pollution. Okay. Technically, runoff is pollution, but we'll add it to the list. Mr. Dorr waited for more answers, but the class was quiet. "Let's add fungi, bacteria, and viruses," he told them, writing.

"Those aren't pollution, Mr. Dorr," said Miguel's twin, Marcos.

"No, you're right. But they're probably caused by, or increased by, pollutants. And they're probably affecting the frogs, which absorb whatever's in their environment through their skin. There's something else that's causing these pollutants' growth. Any ideas?

Remember, it can be a theory. It doesn't have to be proven. Good scientists make educated guesses, then test them out. That's called a hypothesis."

Jackson was raising his hand again, and to his surprise, so was CK. *Call on me. Me! Me! Me!*

"CK?"

Really? Jackson thought. To his amazement, CK responded, "UV light."

"UV light. This is a great example of a theory."

"Not just a theory, Mr. Dorr. In the laboratory, UV light has been proven to cause deformities," Jackson said, then realized he'd been so intent, he hadn't raised his hand before speaking, but Mr. Dorr was cool with it.

"Good, Jackson. To the surprise of Jackson and the whole class, Mr. Dorr turned to CK and nodded. CK went to stand beside Mr. Dorr, who retrieved a biker hat from his desk and put on a pair of sunglasses. Beginning with a little side to side dance move, and clapping in rhythm, they began to chant in unison:

"Vitamin D's a good thing. We get it from the sun.
But too much sun can harm you, if your tan gets overdone.
The Ultraviolet rays, (UV rays, for short)
Can really cause you trouble, and so we will exhort..."

In seconds, Jackson's mouth went from wide open, to a wide grin, matching all the faces in the room. Everyone began to clap. CK and Mr. Dorr continued:

"Use sunscreen! Use sunscreen!"

With this, they leaned into the audience, forward on one foot with one arm stretched out in front, the other behind. As they began their second verse, everyone in the class was rocking from side to side.

"The ozone can protect us; It keeps the UVs out
But holes are being 'eaten,' by fossil fuels, no doubt.
And so, the poor amphibians, like frog and salamander
Are suffer-ing at human hands, we've really raised their dander."

By this time, the kids were standing.

"Use sunscreen! Use sunscreen!"

On, they rapped:

> They live on land and water and they surely do absorb
> Whatever be-comes toxic, when hit by that big orb."

Here, they pointed skyward.

"Use sunscreen! Use sunscreen!"

Mr. Door pointed two fingers at the class, and they all repeated, "Use sunscreen! Use sunscreen!"

They began their last verse:

> "They have no sunscreen, shades, or hats,
> And now they're turning freaky.
> So take their cue for a healthy you:
> Protection's cool, not geeky!"

This time, the class didn't have to be cued. Everyone shouted, "Use sunscreen! Use sunscreen!"

The rap was a huge hit and the class wanted a repeat performance. Mr. Dorr lifted some papers from his desk and handed half to CK. They passed out the rap words to all the kids. When they were ready, CK stood and faced the class, announcing, "UV Rap, by Mr. Dorr."

This time everyone rapped, with some exaggerating movement, competing with each other.

Finally, the class settled back into their seats, and Mr. Dorr asked the class for a round of applause for CK.

"For Mr. Dorr, too. He wrote it." CK graciously told the class.

Replacing his hat and glasses, Mr. Dorr sat on the front of the desk. The class quieted, waiting to hear what had caused their teacher's demeanor to change. He began, "Using sunscreen is, overall, a good thing. But not all sunscreens are created equal. Lately, well, over the last couple of years, some studies have reported problems with the chemicals in some of them."

"Oh, geez! We're gonna' have to become nocturnal," blurted Barry, gaining a fist bump across the aisle from CK.

"No, no, no. This is just a good time to remind ourselves it's important to read labels. There are two basic kinds of sunscreens: Mineral and chemical. Check out your sunscreens at home. The mineral kinds are effective and very safe. They have zinc or titanium dioxide."

"Is that that white stuff?" Jeannine asked.

"Yes, zinc oxide."

"Ew. I've seen people at the beach with that on their noses. Talk about geeky!" CK said.

"Ah! I thought protection's cool, not geeky," Mr. Dorr answered, which caused some conversation among the students. "What's worse? Looking geeky for a little while, or going home with a sunburn and maybe, down the road, skin cancer?" He walked to the board and wrote:

OXYBENZONE

"This is one of the main chemicals found to be harmful. We all can – make that, we all should read labels. Let's make that a goal. That's a bonus assignment. Optional." Mr. Dorr looked at the clock. "Our required assignment? How about tonight we try to discover what we can do about that ozone problem. Look, too, for what changes have been made already in our society. I've been kind of easy on you lately. I want something in writing this time," he said, which inspired several groans.

There were a few minutes left before the bell. The students scrambled to make notes on the assignment, while at the same time, excitedly discussed what they'd learned. CK had become the center of attention. When the bell finally rang, everyone piled out, some reciting the rap as they headed down the hall. To Jackson's surprise CK, who had hung back, grabbed his shoulder, turning him. Before CK had a chance to speak, Jackson blurted, "The rap was great, CK. I didn't know you knew so much stuff about science."

CK's face turned red. "Yeah, well, I don't. I never thought I could be smart like you, so… The room was quiet with Mr. Dorr seated at his desk, and just the two boys, who faced each other. "I guess you think I'm a jerk."

Jackson's eyes raised at that. "No, I don't. You're fun."

Looking at the floor, CK said, "Well, I try really hard to be. I guess I thought if I'm funny, nobody would think I'm stupid."

I'm not the only one! Before Jackson could respond, the second bell rang. CK raised his hand and Jackson responded to the high five. Turning to leave, CK said, "Better get a move on. Stay cool!" By this time, he was out the door and called from the hallway, "I mean, stay in the shade."

He thinks I'm smart. Although he was late, Jackson ambled out the door, deep in thought.

Jackson couldn't wait to get out of school and tell Raina and his parents all about this new wrinkle in the frog chronicles. And check the cabinet for sunscreen chemicals. *What was that called?* He thought. *Oxy – oxybenzone. I'm definitely catching up with Raina in the vocabulary department.*

On the bus ride home, a couple of kids were singing the rap. The bus driver threatened to pull over if they didn't stay in their seats. Jackson and Raina joined in the singing but didn't stand.

The noise was louder than ever, but even the bus driver looked like she was enjoying herself, catching bits and pieces of the conversation, as some of Jackson's classmates shared the rap.

Chapter 12

Cow Poop?

In class the next day, Ray, whom Jackson admired as the best dancer in the school, was raising his hand even before the attendance was taken. By the time Mr. Dorr had finished and looked up, he was eagerly waving his arm in the air. Finally, the teacher called his name.

"Mr. Dorr, I get it that UV light is causing skin cancer, and making stuff in the frogs' environment harmful, but does that mean if we don't protect ourselves, UV light is going to make us have kids with extra or missing arms or legs?"

Jackson knew the answer already. Mr. Dorr shook his head. "I didn't mean to scare you. No, that's not going to happen. But you're right. UV light does cause skin cancer in humans. So avoid getting sunburned. Yes, sunburns are not cool. And protect your eyes.

"Now, as for the frogs...Both organic and manmade stuff becomes toxic, or poisonous when exposed to UV light. If you lived in that stuff, and absorbed it, well, yes, I guess it would affect you. And maybe your offspring."

Jackson raised his hand. "Dr. Thomson said there are experiments going on now, at his university and in other labs, where they're shining UV light on frogs' habitat, stuff like algae and water, and it's causing abnormalities in the frogs."

"So that means the theory has been tested and proven. Thanks, Jackson. So, what are these harmful pollutants? Tara?"

"Oil from cars and trucks?"

"Ah, yes. Major runoff from our roads. Anything else?"

Tara continued, "Spraying for bugs and weeds."

"Yes, pesticides, and herbicides," Mr. Dorr said. "And let's not forget fertilizers."

Jackson sat up straight. He could hardly keep from waving his hand in the air.

Mr. Dorr called, "Jackson? You have another?"

"Cow poop."

Mr. Dorr looked at him and smiled, while the class giggled. CK had taken off the sunglasses he was still wearing and turned around to look at him with what Jackson thought was an admiring look.

"Cow poop," Mr. Dorr repeated, after the hubbub died down. "Well, actually, you're quite right."

"I didn't think of it when Dr. Thomson told me they were surveying to see which had more effect on the creek, the old cattle ranch or the new housing development. But then my dad and I went exploring. There were a lot of cows on that ranch, so there must have been a lot of cow poop." Jackson's face turned slightly pink as he remembered how he'd checked the bottom of his shoe when he and Dad crossed the field to explore the barn.

"And you think the runoff from the ranch harmed the creek?"

"I don't know." Jackson paused. "My neighbors buy big yellow bags of cow manure for the plants in their greenhouse. If it's good for plants, how could it be bad for a creek?"

"That's an excellent observation, Jackson. Nitrogen is a good thing. All life needs it. But too much of any good thing can turn bad. Waste from animals and humans can be bad in large amounts.

"You guys need to stop peeing in the woods!" CK commented.

That was just too good for CK to pass up, Jackson thought.

Ignoring CK, Mr. Dorr continued, "Well, unfortunately, we're all responsible for too much nitrate. In the suburbs, some of the newer housing developments aren't all hooked into the sewer system, and human waste is seeping into the soil from septic tanks, then down into the aquifer where our drinking water is, or into waterways."

A chorus arose: Ew!" "Gross!" "Yuk!" By now, CK was standing, choking himself and gagging.

Jackson was quiet. He remembered Dr. Thomson telling him about the septic tanks in the old houses. He was surprised to know not all new ones were on the sewer line. While chatter went on around him he thought, *if frogs live in the water and absorb chemicals…Poor frogs hardly stand a chance.*

* * *

The next day, when Jackson entered the classroom, he saw Mr. Dorr's desk had been pushed to the front corner of the room. Several students were gathered around Morgan and Miranda, who were on their knees in the open space. They had spread a large roll of blank newsprint. Mr. Dorr was standing over them, along with several students. As more students entered, the space became more crowded, until Mr. Dorr said, "Okay, everybody, let's all take a seat. You, too, girls," he told Morgan and Miranda.

The bell rang and the class settled down. After he took attendance, Mr. Dorr stood and said, "Morgan and Miranda have an interesting proposal." He nodded to the girls. "Come on up front and tell the class your idea."

"We thought it would be fun to make a mural of frogs," Miranda said.

"Why don't you tell the class where your idea came from and maybe a little about what a mural is," Mr. Dorr suggested.

"Okay," Morgan started. "In art class, we made a big mural. The class did it as a group project."

"And what is a mural?" Mr. Dorr asked.

"Well, basically, it's a giant picture painted on the wall. We didn't paint a wall, but a real mural is done on plaster," Morgan said.

"On a really big wall," Miranda added. "Or a ceiling. You know, like Michelangelo painted on the Sistine Chapel."

"We could paint the ceiling in the lobby," CK suggested. "Frogs on clouds! It would really brighten up the place."

"That is one of the reasons people paint murals. To beautify a neighborhood," Mr. Dorr said. What are some other reasons?" he asked.

There was no response. Mr. Dorr prompted, "Do you think a big painting could motivate people to think about something? A social or political issue?"

"Barry sat up. "I know! We could paint a sunny day with a bunch of frogs at the beach sitting under big umbrellas. People would talk about that!"

"Frogs on clouds and frogs on the beach! We need to decide if we want this to be realistic or fun," a student said.

"Good idea. Let's think this through," Mr. Dorr said. "Does the mural have to be completely realistic? We want to make people think, but we can have some fun with it, too. Let your creativity flow. And I think Barry's right. People would sure talk about frogs under an umbrella. It might inspire some conversation about those harmful UV rays."

"Or we could paint frogs with two heads or six legs," said CK.

Mr. Dorr turned to Miranda and asked, "Does a mural have to be just a single scene?"

"Oh, no. Sometimes it is, but sometimes it's a lot of scenes, all on one canvas–or one wall."

Morgan was nodding her head. "We could do whatever we want."

"So we could have frogs on the ceiling and they could rain down the walls." CK insisted.

Jackson was thinking, He's *getting carried away* when Mr. Dorr, who had been walking back and forth across the newly opened space, stopped in his tracks and stood looking at CK. Directing his question at his student, Mr. Dorr asked, "Can it rain frogs?"

CK answered, "My Dad said there was a movie where it rained frogs."

"But that doesn't make it a real thing," said another student.

"Actually, it is a real thing," Mr. Dorr said. This had the classes' attention. There was no talking, even from CK. "There are well-documented cases of animal rain."

"Oh, yeah. People say, 'It rained cats and dogs!'" came from the back of the room.

CK missed that one, Jackson thought.

Mr. Dorr continued, "Back as far as the fourth century BC there are reports of it raining fish and frogs. I remember a report of frogs raining for three days. The people had to leave the town where it occurred. Let me see…" Mr. Dorr went to the computer near where his desk usually was. "It was in Turkey." Facing the class again, he continued, "There are numerous reports of it raining frogs or fish. I recall it happening as recently as 2005, somewhere in Europe." He bent over the computer again. "Yes, in Serbia, thousands of frogs rained. And in Memphis, once, there were live snakes."

"Aii! Could that ever happen here?" Jeannine asked, competing with several other protests.

"Well, I suppose it's possible, but I doubt it. Obviously, it doesn't happen often. Let's figure out how it happens. Think about CK's cloud frogs. How could frogs get into the clouds?"

Of course, CK had an answer. "They're really good hoppers!"

There were a couple of giggles. "Not that good," Mr. Dorr said. "All right, then. What makes clouds?"

"Evaporation." came from more than one student. "Water," from another.

"Correct," said Mrs. Dorr. "Clouds form when water heats up and evaporates, then rises to form clouds."

"So the frogs and snakes evaporate and get to the clouds," CK said.

Several kids had comments about that, directed at CK. Some weren't especially nice. He's *just trying to be funny* Jackson thought.

Looking directly at CK, Mr. Dorr said, "You know only liquid evaporates. So no, CK, that's not how they got into the sky." Scanning the class, he asked, "What's another way something could get into the air above us? Think."

"Wind?" someone asked.

"Now you're thinking. What's another weather phenomenon?" the teacher asked. "Here's a hint: It involves both wind and water."

"My grandparents were in a hurricane in Florida and they said water caused more damage than the wind. Is it a hurricane?"

"No, but you're getting closer," Mr. Dorr answered. When met with silence, he said, "Have you heard of a waterspout?" There was chatter about that. Mr. Dorr continued. "Remember what the tornado does."

A few seconds passed before a boy in the front row asked, "Can a tornado pick up water?" "If frogs were in the water, then…"

Mr. Dorr was nodding. "Go on."

The boy continued, "Tornados pick up stuff. So, if a tornado picked up water, couldn't it pick up what's in it? Like fish and frogs?"

"Bingo!" Mr. Dorr walked to the board and quickly drew a tornado shape. Turning back to the class, he said, "If a tornado sucks things up and transports them somewhere else…you tell me…" He could see it was dawning on several faces, as hands shot up.

"Jackson?"

Jackson answered, "Then a water spout is just a tornado with water in it?" Mr. Dorr smiled and Jackson continued, "Water it got from a lake or river."

"Yep! If a tornado forms over a shallow pond, say, not more than three feet deep, it could certainly pick up water – and anything in it."

"Why just frogs?" someone asked.

"Ah, a good question. People have seen it rain frogs, fish, tadpoles or jellyfish…"

"Don't forget snakes," Jeannine reminded him.

"Ah, yes. Snakes. Notice mostly aquatic organisms. People have seen it raining animals, but no one's ever actually seen a waterspout pick up the critters. Yet…" Glancing at the clock, he said, "We've kind of gotten off track and we're running out of time.

"Could we incorporate everybody's ideas into the mural? CK's cloud frogs and Barry's beach frogs?" Mr. Dorr asked.

Both girls answered in the affirmative.

"I think this is a project that will take a little planning. First we'll have to get permission from Principal Brewer, but I happen to know he's something of an amateur artist himself, so I think we may find he'll support our idea."

There was excitement, as everyone wanted to share their ideas with each other. "I tell you what," said Mr. Dorr. "How about tonight, everyone come up with an idea for what you want to include in the mural. You can work together with a buddy, if you like. We'll follow Miranda's suggestion that it can be many pictures in one."

Morgan raised her hand. "Yes, Morgan?"

"We should all do a sketch of what we want to put in the mural and then put them all together."

"That's a great idea. Then we'll have a plan to show Mr. Brewer. Something else we need to think about: Michelangelo didn't fund that ceiling. He had sponsors." Mr. Dorr told them. "We're going to need sponsors, too. Paint isn't free. Be thinking about possible sources of funding."

Chapter 13

Target Practice

"W"ANNA come over?" Jackson asked Raina on the bus. "I thought I might go down to the creek."

"Sure thing. Right after I check in with Mom," Raina answered, just as the bus pulled to a stop. "See you in a few!"

Jackson was already outside when Raina arrived and parked her bike. "Is Dr. Thomson going with us?" she asked.

"I don't know. Didn't see him yesterday or today. Let's cut through his yard to the creek. Maybe he's outside." They stepped through the hole in the hedge and saw him, just as he let a small missile go from a slingshot. The kids hurried to his side.

"Wow, that's pretty cool, Dr. T.," Jackson said.

"Why, haven't you ever seen this ole' thing?"

Jackson shook his head.

"I figured I had plenty more rubber, now that you found my other boot, so I had to come up with a practical way to recycle it. This one's old, so I replaced the sling, which was pretty worn."

"You made this slingshot?"

Dr. Thomson nodded. "A long time ago."

"You must have a lot of rubber left over, Dr. Thomson," Raina said.

"Well, now that you mention it, I did." Reaching around to his back, Dr. Thomson pulled two more slingshots from his back pockets and handed one to each of the kids.

Holding onto the wooden handle, they both pulled several times on the rubber part of the sling. "I'm not sure my mom will let me have this," Raina said.

"Ah! A good point. I did ask your folks, Jackson, before I offered, but I haven't had a chance to call your mom, Raina. We'll remedy that this evening. In the meantime, let's have a lesson. It's important to be responsible and not misuse tools."

"Tools? Isn't this a weapon?" Jackson asked. "David killed Goliath with a slingshot."

"Yes, he did. But think about it. What else could you do with this?"

"Hunt?"

"You sure could. Personally, I use it to hunt cherries. The most delectable member of the rose family."

"Cherries?" Jackson and Raina both asked at the same time.

"Cherries. See that small tree?" he asked, pointing. "Watch." Dr. Thomson placed a small stone into the sling and shot towards the tree.

"Wow. But you didn't get any cherries," Jackson said.

"You don't think? Let's go see. They're not ripe, yet, but they're big enough for me to hit. I'm a pretty good shot," Dr. Thomson told them, as they walked over and searched under the place where the stone had struck.

"Well, I'll be!" Raina said, picking up a cherry. "You didn't hit the cherry. You hit the stem and knocked it down."

Jackson looked up at the tree. "That's amazing, Dr. T. What were you shooting at before? It wasn't cherries."

"True. A rabbit was raiding vegetable patch, nibbling at the tender new shoots."

Raina was silent, but Jackson said, "Oh, Dr. T., I thought you only hunted cherries," which sounded kind of silly after he said it, but Jackson didn't care, because he was upset.

"Oh, I wouldn't hit the rabbit. I struck the ground between him and a cabbage. The kids knew that was quite possible for Dr. Thomson, after seeing him shoot the cherry stem.

"Oh, well, then. Can we try it?" Jackson asked.

"Of course. I've set up a small target over here." As they walked to the target, Dr. Thomson said, "Unless you're planning on eating an animal, it wouldn't be responsible to shoot it." He stopped and tapped his forehead with the heel of his hand. "We could shoot frogs."

Incredulous, Jackson said, "But that would kill them."

"Dinner!" answered Dr. Thomson.

As they came within sight of the target, Jackson said, "You're joking, right? Who would eat frogs for dinner?"

"I would," Dr. Thomson answered. "At least the legs."

Since nothing about Dr. Thomson would surprise Jackson, he dropped the subject. Anyway, they had arrived at the target. Jackson and Raina took turns shooting, with Dr. Thomson's guidance, and each managed several hits.

"Not bad," said Dr. Thomson. "Say, why are frogs happy?"

Jackson was thinking, *Happy? Seems like frogs are unhappy to me,* when Dr. Thomson said, "They can eat whatever bugs them."

Reminded of frogs, Jackson said, "Oh, Dr. T., I almost forgot! We have a rap for you."

"A rap? Is that a kind of music?"

"Sort of. We learned this in science class today. Well, I did. Raina learned it on the bus."

Raina took the paper from her pocket and unfolded it. "I don't know all the words yet," she explained.

Dr. Thomson nodded. "I'll just sit here," he said, as he sat down on a bench to listen. When they finished the rap, Dr. Thomson clapped, then told them, "You could do a lot of good with that rap. You need to take it on the road. I can see your name in lights, now: *Raina and Jackson, the Sun Screamin' Kids.*"

"Nah, I don't think so." Jackson could see CK on stage, but not himself.

"Your rap is great. But remember, UV is only part of frogs' problems," Dr. T. said, as he tossed a weed into his bucket." Probably their biggest threat now is a fungus called Chytrid."

"Geesh! What next? Frogs sure are having a rough time," Raina said.

"Well, think about it. There are a thousand different Chytrid species which live in water and moist environments."

"Just like frogs!" Jackson said.

"Yep. And if you have permeable skin, you soak up everything in the water."

"Guess sunscreen won't protect them from that," Jackson's mournful face followed Dr. Thomson's, as he rose up with his bucket.

"Well, Dr. T., we're going down to the creek to check on the frogs and fish."

"And boots," Raina added, to the laughter of all. "Want to go with us?"

"Thanks, but not today, my friends. I'm going to finish weeding my vegetable garden, then I have to clean up for class tonight. Say, what's a frog's favorite kind of music?"

"Hmmm…I know it's not opera. Rock? They like to sit on rocks in the creek," Raina guessed.

"Well, it *is* contemporary."

Jackson found himself tensing up, determined to get the answer before Raina. "I know! I know! Hip hop!"

Raina twisted her head, looking sideways at him. "Very cool."

At that, Jackson swelled, lowering his head so his red face didn't show.

Dr. Thomson put a hand on Jackson's shoulder. "You guys be careful. If you see any storm trooper boots out there, come and get me."

"Will do." Distracted, Jackson smiled. Heading for the creek, Raina asked, "Storm trooper boots?"

"Didn't you ever see those Star Wars movies?" Jackson asked.

"Oh, yeah," Raina answered, giggling. "I really like Dr. T., but he's kind of strange."

"In a good way," Jackson replied.

"Oh, for sure," Rania agreed. By this time, they were at the creek. Jackson set down the habitat and Raina handed him one of the nets. "Careful. Let's not slip."

"Nope. Don't wanna do a Dr. T.," Jackson said, which made them both laugh.

The kids quieted, advancing a few feet at a time. Jackson crouched, his head moving slowly from wide left to right. Whap!

"Did you get one?" Raina called.

"Naw. Missed him. I moved too fast. Gotta be sneakier." It took a while before either sighted another frog. Jackson leaned forward, intently scanning the creek. When Raina caught the first one, Jackson gritted his teeth and wiped his palms on the side of his pants, but said, "Good going!"

Jackson was beginning to get discouraged, when he saw a frog on the bank. "Raina, come here! Come see this," he whispered. But Raina didn't answer. Shaking with excitement, Jackson knew he had to be stealthy and not rush this time. He inched closer to the frog. Slowly, he lowered his arm, then, whap! "Got you!"

"Raina, Raina, come see this!" He shouted this time, to be sure she heard him over the sound of the creek. As he climbed the bank, he held the hind legs of the frog through the net.

Raina got to the habitat just as Jackson was shaking the frog from the net into the carrier. "Whoa! A freaky frog. Jackson, you got yourself a freaky frog!"

Jackson lifted the habitat so they could get a better look. Neither said anything, both lost in thought. Finally, Jackson said, "I hope Dr. T. isn't in the shower, yet."

"I thought your parents didn't want you to go into his house anymore." Raina said. "They're going to freak when they find out you touched a freaky frog."

"Oh, once they found out we can't get sick from the frogs, they were okay with it."

To their disappointment, Dr. T. was no longer in the yard. They climbed the stairs to the porch and knocked on the back door. After a moment, Dr. Thomson opened the door and Jackson thrust the habitat into his face. "Look, Dr. T.!"

Carrying the case to a porch chair, Dr. T. sat and studied Jackson's frog. "Well, well, well." When he said no more, Jackson asked, "What happened to him, Dr. T.? What's happening to the creek? Do you think there are more? What should we do with him?"

"Slow down, there. One thing at a time. Tell me, now, do frogs have tails? That is, do frogs normally have tails?"

Both children shook their heads. "No, but tadpoles do," Raina said.

"Bingo. What's happened here is the tail wasn't absorbed as metamorphosis occurred. As the tadpole changed form, the tail should have disappeared."

"Does that mean the creek is polluted?"

"I don't think so. It's actually been improving steadily the last couple of years since the ranch was converted into a housing development. This is probably just an anomaly. I don't think it's an indication that there are still too many nitrates or other pollutants in the riparian area. We actually found more frogs like this little guy, several years ago."

"What should we do with him, Dr. T.?" Raina asked.

"Good question. We'll certainly document this. First, I want to take a picture," Dr. Thomson said, rising to go inside. "Come on in."

Dr. Thomson placed a white board in an empty tank. "Put him in there, Jackson. They never smile when they pose for a picture. Guess they're unhoppy."

"That's pretty bad, Dr. T."

"Yeah, sometimes I can't help myself. Say 'cheese', little guy," Dr. T. said, as he aimed the camera. After taking the picture, he replaced the frog into Jackson's habitat. "Now we need to record a few things. Can you show me exactly where you found him?"

They headed back to the creek, clipboard in hand. Jackson was surprised that Dr. Thomson had given him the frog. "Aren't you going to keep him, Dr. T.? For your studies?"

"I know you'd like to have him to show your family, J, but I'd like to ask you to hold off taking him to school."

"Can I at least tell them about it?"

"Well, eventually, sure. But for now, until our survey is done, let's keep him at home. We don't want every kid in the county taking frogs from this creek. It will skew the data. Let's be discreet."

Jackson nodded. He didn't even have to think about Dr. Thomson's use of a word he had never heard before. "Got it!"

* * *

When Jackson entered class the next day, he was surprised at his feelings. It was hard to sit still. He kept taking deep breaths. *Why am I doing this? It's like the words want to jump out of my mouth but all I can let out is air!* The discussion was, of course, about the mural. Jackson could hardly concentrate. His thoughts were still on his freaky frog at home, but he knew he couldn't share it. Yet. *Maybe I'll just tell Mr. Dorr after class.*

The class was debating whether to confine the mural contents to native frogs or allow exotics. Miranda was lobbying for exotics' inclusion. She really wanted to include her favorite, the Tomato frog.

Finally, Brian sealed the deal when he argued that frogs worldwide were under siege, not just local ones.

"Now that we've settled that," Mr. Dorr said, "I have some good news. Mrs. Bast, the art teacher has agreed to supervise the project. Those who can, will meet with her after school tomorrow for instructions."

Taking one more deep breath, Jackson relaxed. Well, maybe it'll take my mind off the frogs at home, if I can work on frogs at school, he told himself.

Chapter 14

We're on TV!

SEVERAL days later, Jackson and the class were surprised when Mr. Dorr announced they would be going on a mini field trip. A murmur ran through the class. "To see frogs?" Jeannine asked.

"To see frogs," Mr. Dorr answered. "We're going to the Media Center."

A chorus of "Aws" rang out.

Mr. Dorr held up his hands. "Wait a minute! Trust me on this. Jackson's neighbor, Dr. Thomson, a prominent herpetologist at the university, has agreed to make a visit to the school.

We'll be joining him in the Media Center, where he'll show us some of his frogs."

"His freaky frogs?" Barry asked.

"His freaky frogs. Jackson, will you bring yours, too? The presentation will be broadcast Friday morning over the school's in-house TV station, so the entire school can see it."

"But we'll get to see them live, and in person!" CK declared.

"Yes. And also, live and in person, will be the Freaky Frog Rap."

"We're going to do the rap on TV?" CK asked.

"Yes, that is, if everyone agrees. I thought, since you all know it so well, the entire class could do it."

Everyone began talking at once. Raising his hands again, Mr. Dorr continued, "We'll do a practice run today, but tape tomorrow, during class time. So, instead of reporting here for class, go directly to the Media Center. Oh, and if you want to wear sunglasses, just for the performance, feel free," which caused another round of chatter.

"Jackson, would you give, maybe a two-sentence summary of what's being done to help the ozone and the frogs?"

Jackson felt a wave of panic come over him. "Me? On TV?"

"Sure. Just tell them about the chemicals we used to use in aerosol cans and refrigeration, that are no longer manufactured. And tell them to pull weeds by hand, instead of using spray and not to use fertilizers near streams and ponds. Can you do that?"

Two sentences, Jackson thought. "I guess I could."

The next day, Dr. Thomson gave Jackson a ride to school and they carried several aquariums to the Media Center, which was quiet when they entered. Soon Jackson's classmates began to arrive and gathered excitedly around Dr. Thomson's frogs. There was a lot of talk among the students, and Jackson began to relax. As he chatted with his friends, answering their questions about the frogs, he forgot how nervous he'd felt only minutes before.

Every student had dressed up for the presentation. Ray was the envy of all the boys with his biker boots. Morgan surprised everyone with her stylish leather vest and jeans. Almost everyone wore sunglasses and those who didn't, wore hats. Miranda's sunglasses were hot pink. "No surprise, there," Jeannine told Denise, as they both admired their colorful friend's accessories.

Before the taping, CK showed everyone the little dance move. "Now, by the time we get to 'Use sunscreen! Use sunscreen!' you need to be leaning forward on your right foot, stretching your right hand out in front of you," he explained. "Kick your left foot and hand out backwards." For once, everyone took him seriously and listened to his instructions.

Mr. Dorr talked with Dr. Thomson while the kids practiced the move. The bell rang and the kids quieted for the Pledge of Allegiance and news from the principal, then Mr. Dorr asked them to sit together on the floor. When the announcements were over, the media specialist, Mrs. Dimperio, explained how the taping would go.

First, Mr. Dorr introduced Dr. Thomson, who showed his freaky frog collection. Then Dr. T. surprised Jackson by introducing him. Jackson rubbed his hands together and found they were sweaty. He wiped them on his pants and stood. *They can't see my legs wobbling* he told himself, heading to the front.

Before he could open his mouth, Dr. Thomson asked him, "Jackson, what did the frog driver say to the frog hitchhiker?"

That's an easy one, Jackson thought. His whole body relaxed. "Hop in!" Jackson answered, raising laughter from his classmates. Jackson looked out over the room, and relaxed. *They like me,* he realized. Then he explained what the class had learned that was helping heal the ozone and ultimately, the frogs.

Mrs. Dimperio stopped taping while the rest of the class joined Jackson. Brian nudged Jackson. "Great job, Frogman!"

Frogman. I have a nickname. "It was easier than I thought it would be. Boy, was I nervous when I first got here," Jackson answered. Brian gave him a slap on the back.

Mrs. Dimperio gave the signal and they performed the rap. Everyone hammed it up. It was so good that Mrs. Dimperio said they didn't need any more takes.

The presentation was a huge hit, especially the rap. When word spread, the local newspaper came to interview Mr. Dorr and Jackson. The interview was conducted in the lobby of the school, in front of the giant mural Mr. Dorr's class had painted, working after school for about two weeks. The television station picked up the story, and ultimately, the AP picked it up and took it national.

Jackson had painted two of Dr. T's freaky frogs, confined to an aquarium. CK's contribution was obvious to all, a dead frog, his feet in the air, lying in a roadside ditch. Miranda had been right about the addition of colorful exotics. The class had placed her Tomato frog, puffed up in a defensive posture, front and center. Jackson told Raina, "Sometimes I feel like a celebrity when I walk down the hall. Kids I don't know are always stopping me, asking about the frogs."

"Well, you're the Frogman," Raina said.

The end of the school year was comming all too soon for Jackson and his frog friends. "I'm going to hate leaving Mr. Dorr," he told his classmates, who all agreed with him.

When he told Raina, she said, "Maybe I'll get him next year, then I can tell you about class every day." But Jackson knew it just wasn't going to be the same.

The last week of school, Mr. Dorr was elected Teacher of the Year. No one was surprised. As good-byes were said, there was talk of changing the school nickname to the Faraday Frogs. That didn't fly with the administration. Anyway, "The Faraday Freaky Frogs" was really what the kids had hoped for.

Chapter 15

The Bullfrogs

JUNE passed quickly. In July, Jackson and Raina joined Dr. Thomson's survey team, collecting and documenting, in a quest to determine what, and how much harm was being done to the environment. The data would be compared to surveys of the past several years, in areas where housing had replaced farms and ranches. The team worked different areas every day, visiting places they had surveyed in previous years. Jackson and Raina sat in the middle of the van discussing what the team had found. "Well, there were several "freaky frogs," said Raina.

"I don't know," answered Jackson. "Do frogs whose tails have not been absorbed qualify as freaky?"

"Your standards have changed, J," Dr. Thomson said. You thought the first tailed frog you found back in May was pretty freaky." He had adopted his own nickname for Jackson since the survey had started.

Jackson kind of liked it. *In a way, it makes us like equals. Dr. T. and J. Maybe someday, Dr. J.*

"Oh, I know a tailed frog is unusual. And that it means something's wrong, but…"

"You were kind of hoping to find some frogs with six legs."

"Well, yeah, I guess so. But I know it would mean bad things were happening to the creek if we did," said Jackson.

By the last day of the survey, the team was a considerable distance from Dr. Thomson's backyard. They had actually driven to a site close to the place where the creek emptied into the larger Faraday River. Around four o'clock the group had gathered near the van. Some of the grad students were organizing materials on a portable table they'd set up, and packing equipment.

"Well, we've covered a lot of area this week. So, how did you like being surveyors?" Dr. Thomson asked.

"It was great! I didn't know the creek was so big," Raina said.

"Oh, yes, it's pretty long. It's about fifteen miles from Jackson's house and mine to the river," Dr. Thomson said. "And it goes a couple of miles in the other direction. Listen, we're going to knock off a little early today. We've accomplished a lot."

"Aw. We haven't found any really freaky frogs," Jackson said.

"But that's a good thing. We should be hoppy."

"Hoppy?" Raina asked.

"Frog aficionados, that is, fans, are either hoppy or sad," Dr. T. said, as he slung his backpack into the van.

"Oh, geez," Jackson said, shaking his head.

"Remember why we're doing this," said Bill, one of Dr. Thomson's grad students.

"Oh, yeah, I know," answered Jackson. "To find frogs you tagged before."

"And?" asked Dr. Thomson.

"And tag more," Raina said.

"And see what the frogs are telling us about the environment," Jackson added.

"Very good, J. Now, since we've got a little daylight left, Bill suggested you guys do a little exploring with him and Stacy. That is, if you want to."

Both Jackson and Raina jumped up from where they were seated on the ground, and the four took off, waving to Dr. T., who was already helping his other students load equipment into the van.

"Hey, Bill, what's green and goes one hundred miles an hour?" Jackson asked.

Stacy and Bill both laughed. "You've been hanging around Dr. T. too long. You're starting to sound like him."

Jackson's head moved slowly from left to right. "Guess you already heard that one."

"Well, I haven't," said Raina. "What's green and goes one hundred miles an hour?"

Bill and Stacy were quiet, so Jackson told her, "A frog in a blender."

Raina wrinkled her nose and everyone laughed. Then Raina said, "If you added milk and eggs, you could make frog nog."

Everyone groaned. Bill grinned at Stacy and said, "I think she's one of us." Jackson nodded.

The path was slightly rolling, with ups and downs. They reached a portion of the trail which rose steeply. "Gee, we should have done this first thing in the morning, before we were so tired," Stacy said.

They climbed without talking, though not without some panting. Reaching the summit, they stopped to rest and drink some water. The sun was lower in the sky now and they were in shadows. "Mmm. This coolness feels good," Raina said.

"We should probably start back down. I had hoped we could go farther. The path goes downward again and then it's smooth sailing to the river," Bill said.

"But we'd have to climb back up this hill again," said Stacy.

"Yep."

Just then, there was a loud, deep sound which Jackson knew was a frog, but not one he'd ever heard.

"Rumm, rumm, rumm. Rumm, rumm, rumm."

"What is that?" Raina asked.

Jackson noticed that Bill and Stacy had stopped and looked at each other. "It's a bullfrog. He's close by. Stand still."

"Rumm, Rumm, Rumm," came the sound.

"I mostly hear frogs at night. Is this unusual?" Jackson whispered.

Bill crept to the edge of the path and parted some brush.

"Not so much, and the sun is starting to go down," Stacy answered. "They have a variety of calls. Sometimes an alarm call, which we may have inspired. You do hear them in the evening and at night, but you'll hear them more during mating season."

They watched, as Bill stooped and parted the branches of a bush. "Whoa!" Jackson said. "He's humongous! I've never seen a frog that big."

"Open the bag," Bill said to Stacy. He leaned towards the frog and managed to catch it.

"We're going to keep it?" Raina asked.

"Oh, you bet we are. Wait 'till Dr. T. sees this. He's gonna croak!" Bill said, stuffing the bullfrog into the bag Stacy carried.

Jackson could see by the look on Bill's face, and Stacy's, too, that this was no joke.

"Do you think there are more like him?" Jackson asked.

"Oh, probably," Bill answered.

"Unfortunately," Stacy added.

The group walked quietly, Raina and Jackson in front, with the grad students bringing up the rear. Unable to remain silent for very long, Jackson asked, "Is he a freaky frog? He's awfully big."

"He's not freaky, but he's freaking me out," Stacy said. "Bullfrogs can be as large as eight and a half inches long. They can move nine and a half kilometers. That's about six miles in a few weeks."

"And that's bad?" Raina asked.

"Well... Not in some areas, but they're new here. The other amphibians around here probably aren't happy about it," answered Bill.

They had traveled faster on their return trip and were approaching the van, where Dr. T. stood waiting for them.

"What aren't amphibians happy about? asked Dr. Thomson. Stacy removed the bullfrog from her bag and handed him to Dr. Thomson.

"Aw. How many?"

"Don't know. He's the only one we saw, but where there's one…"

"There are more," finished Dr. Thomson. "Guess we'll be back tomorrow. Placing the frog in a container, he handed it back to Stacy and said, "You can write him up on the way home. Okay, everybody, load 'em up!"

Chapter 16

A Frog Chorus

As they climbed into the van, Jackson asked, "How do you know it's a him?"

"Beginning mating season. Females have a smooth white neck. This guy's green," answered Bill.

It was pretty quiet in the van. Bill helped Stacy measure the bullfrog.

Jackson watched her take its temperature and swab it. Bill said, "We'll check it for chytrid back at the lab."

"Are you going to put a PIT tag in him?" Jackson asked.

"Not in this baby! We're not going to release him again," Bill said.

"Are they bad for the environment?"

"Well, it depends on where you find them. They're not really bad for their stabilized natural habitat, but they're new to this neighborhood."

"They're pretty loud, too," Jackson said.

"Yeah, they are. City slickers might consider them noise polluters," Bill half joked.

Nobody acted like it was funny, so Jackson didn't laugh. "Why don't you like them?"

"They're cannibals!" Stacy said.

"Huh?"

"Cannibals? Really?" Raina asked. "They eat other frogs?"

From the front of the van, Dr. Thomson explained, "Many animals eat their own kind. And in the bullfrog's defense, there are other frog species that also do. These will eat their own, and other species' tadpoles and the younger, smaller bullfrogs. It's not easy for smaller amphibians, who aren't genetically programmed, to avoid and survive these giants."

Everyone rode without speaking for about half a minute, then Stacy said, "They move quickly. As soon as they can get away from their parents and other large bullfrogs, they hop off into the distance.

"They're widespread east of the Rockies, but to the west, only in coastal areas where they've been introduced. So it was only a matter of time before they reached our neck of the woods."

"And that's bad." Raina said.

Stacy answered, "Bad for the other frogs in this region. Bullfrogs often take over other frogs' habitat and eat what they would be eating. They're yucky and their tadpoles are yucky. Fish will eat other frogs' tadpoles, but they won't eat bullfrog tadpoles because they're yucky." Looking down at the frog, she repeated, "Yucky, yucky, yucky!"

"Wait a minute!" Angie, another student said. "I've eaten frog legs and they're delicious!"

"Were they bullfrog legs?" Jackson asked.

And Bill teased, "Did they taste like chicken?"

Angie made a face at him. "No, they're kind of fishy."

"That figures," Bill said.

"They might have been bullfrogs' legs. I did eat them in California" Angie thought for a minute. "People there have been eating them for a long time. They actually import them to satisfy the demand for frog legs."

Kerry chimed in. "I heard there's a movement in California to stop importation of frogs' legs. It's actually banned in one county."

"Why did they change their minds?" Raina asked.

Oh, not everybody did. But some people are recognizing the eco-logical damage an aggressive species like the bullfrog can cause. And how harmful they are to native species. They could be transporting chytrid fungus with the frogs."

"That's California," piped the student in the back. "Always in the forefront. First to import frog legs, now first to ban them."

"People import bullfrogs to eat? Really?" Jackson asked.

"Yep," the student answered.

"Where do they come from?" Raina asked.

Bill finished documenting the frog and joined the conversation. "They're native to North America and now they're found throughout the world."

"Yes," said Stacy. "They're leaping around the world. Sometimes people help by letting exotics like bullfrogs loose. And exotics usually have no native predators."

"Why would people do that?" Raina asked.

Dr. Thomson had been listening to the conversation. "Well, right here in Idaho, bullfrogs are established in only a few areas, but some nurseries were selling bullfrog tadpoles. People like to have them in their backyard ponds. They didn't know it was illegal to own or sell them or their tadpoles, so now Division of Wildlife Resource agents are working to find customers who bought tadpoles from those nurseries.

"Here in the west, our native predators, like eagles and snakes, might feed occasionally on young bullfrogs, but it's not enough to stop the influx." The mood had turned somber, so Doctor T. asked, "Hey, you guys. What do you call a frog with no legs?" Raina and Jackson were sure they were about to learn a new scientific name for the freaky frogs back at Dr. T's house, but the grad students were all smiling.

"He couldn't hop," Dr. T. hinted.

Raina's face lit up. "Unhoppy!" She and Jackson smiled at each other. Jackson's face turned red, and he turned back to face forward.

Several more jokes surfaced. The students competed, sharing their frog jokes with the kids. Eventually things quieted and Jackson asked, "If bullfrogs' legs are so delicious…" He looked to Stacy, but she didn't say anything. "Well, if people in California like them so much…"

"Oh, people throughout the country eat them. I may not like them, but a lot of people do," said Stacy. "If their tadpoles and young are the only ones a bass won't eat, I'm sure not going to eat them!"

"Where do you get them? To eat, I mean. Do they sell them at the grocery store?" asked Raina.

"Sure, in some places." Bill answered. "But you can go frog gigging and get them for free."

"Frog gigging?" Jackson had forgotten his original question.

"First, you need a gig. A long pole with a spike on the end. You go out into a wetland, a swampy area, and take a light," Bill started.

"You need a light? Do you go at night?" Raina asked.

"Yep. Some people go in boats. Some just wear waders and walk in."

The kids were thoughtful. "So, you stick the frog with the spike," Jackson said.

"The gig. Exactly. You can buy a frog gig spear at Bass Pro Shop – they're real cheap – then attach it to a wooden pole or a ten-foot section of conduit." Bill said.

Someone in the back of the van said, "Or just make your own, with some kind of spike, like a really long nail. Voila! You're ready to stab and jab. Then you spindle your catch."

The kids both looked to Bill for confirmation.

He said, "It's called spindling. Just like you put the fish you catch on a line. Easier to carry them home."

"There are some biologists working on a bullfrog removal project right now, here in Idaho. They're using an experimental technique, electrofrogging," Dr. Thomson told them.

"Shocking!" one student said. There was some laughter.

Jackson's ears perked up. "Really? They're shocking frogs?"

"Remember, they're a threat to some native amphibians, like Western toads and Northern leopard frogs.

After another pause, Jackson said, "Oh, I know what I wanted to ask. If frogs are so delicious..." Again, he looked at Stacy, but she said nothing, so he continued. "Why don't they just go out and gig them and sell them to grocery stores and restaurants?"

Another student said, "They sell pickled pigs' feet in gas stations and convenience stores. They should pickle frog's legs and sell them."

This time Jackson's nose wrinkled. "You really think people would buy them?""I don't know if pickled frogs' legs would sell," Bill said. "But some people do go gigging and sell to stores and restaurants. Americans just don't eat them in great enough numbers."

"Too bad," Stacy said. "Think about it. They reproduce like crazy. A female can have from 1000 to 20,000 eggs."

"20,000. Wow," said Raina.

"Yes, wow," said Dr. Thomson. "Over her lifetime, she could lay up to 400,000 eggs."

"Double wow," said Jackson.

"Not only are they outcompeting and eating everything in their path, they're carriers of the fungus, which has wiped out some other species. They seem mostly immune to it, themselves," Stacy added.

"Doesn't look like anything's going to stop the bullfrog," Bill added.

Dr. Thomson said, "No, not likely. Guess we'll have to develop some marketing strategies to sell more frog legs. How about some frog fritters?"

Everyone laughed. The student who was driving said, "Or frog-furters."

Everyone began making suggestions. "Frog fondue," said Angie. Jackson had an idea. "Instead of fudgsicles, frogsicles."

Raina added, "You could use your blender, Dr. T. Instead of berry smoothies, you could make frog frosties." Everyone groaned and Stacy threw in a "Yuk! That'll bring them in!"

"You could offer freeze-dried frogs to the grocery stores, so everyone could have frogs in the freezer. Then you could just pop out a couple at a time for smoothies."

"I think I'm going to be sick," said Stacy.

"Let's open a restaurant that only serves frog food. We'll advertise 'Hoppy Meals' for the kids. What shall we call it?" asked Dr. Thomson.

Everyone had an idea. Forever Frogs seemed to be the winner, "Since it looks like we'll have bullfrogs around forever," Stacy said.

"Unfortunately," Bill said. "Although it could represent our hope for all of Frogdom...that there will be frogs on the planet forever."

"Frogs, but not just bullfrogs," said Jackson. Everyone agreed.

They rode for a while, chatting among themselves about the day's events, then one student began a low "Rummm, rummm, rummm. Giga rummm, rummm."

Stacy leaned over and told Jackson and Raina, "The bullfrog."

Jackson nodded, but then twisted his head to see who had started a high pitched "Peep peep. Peep peep. Peep peep."

"Spring peeper," Stacy said.

Other sounds started up, one at a time. There was a trilling sound. "Gray tree frog," Stacy told them. "Want to join in?" Both nodded enthusiastically. Stacy pointed two index fingers at Raina. "Zzzzzii- iip. Zzzzziiiip." Raina took up the chant.

She pointed at Jackson. "Gonk gunk gunk. Gonk gunk gunk." Jackson repeated once, unsure, but Stacy had started her own song, so he continued.

By the time everyone had taken up a frog call, it was loud, but as soon as everyone was calling, one stopped, then another, then another, until there was only the "Peep peep. Peep peep. Peep peep." Finally, it, too, stopped.

"That was so fun!" Raina's enthusiasm seemed to speak for everyone.

Jackson answered, "Yeah, but so noisy!"

"Just like the wetland at night," someone said.

Jackson laughed. "Or Dr. Thomson's house," Everyone had something to say about that. Finally, Jackson asked, "Dr. T., I was wondering. Do you ever have trouble sleeping, with all those frogs in your house?"

"Oh, no," said Dr. Thomson, just as the driver turned into his driveway. "I have trouble sleeping when I'm in the quiet city!" Jackson smiled, remembering the night sounds from his old apartment in the city—not exactly quiet.

Someone suggested, "You could go to YouTube and enter *bullfrog sounds* or *frog chorus* when you're in the city, and it'll be like you're home, Dr. T."

"I hadn't thought of that," Dr. Thomson answered.

The van came to a stop and Raina and Jackson got out. Dr. Thomson told them, "We're heading back to the lab. I hope we'll see you tomorrow." The students all called goodbyes.

Jackson waved. "See you tomorrow!"

Raina called, "Thank-you!" as the van pulled away.

Chapter 17

A Celebrated Frog

Jackson was hungry at dinnertime, but he could hardly eat, he had so much to tell Mom and Dad. "What kind of shoes does a fashionable amphibian wear?" he asked.

"That's what you learned today?" Dad asked, jokingly.

Jackson was about to put a forkful of mashed potatoes into his mouth, but paused and answered, "That and a lot of other stuff."

"So, how about the shoes?"

"A fashionable frog wears open toad shoes." Jackson grinned, and shoveled the heap of potatoes into his mouth.

"Any more?" Mom asked.

"Always," Jackson mumbled, his mouth full. "What's a frog's favorite time?"

"Spring?" Mom guessed, tapping her mouth.

"Nope. Leap year!" Jackson reached across the table for the plate of pork chops.

"Jackson, we would have passed that. I don't know if letting you hang out in the wilds has done your manners any good," Mom said.

"It's certainly done your appetite some good," Dad laughed.

Jackson told them about the bullfrogs. "I know we were checking for freaky frogs, but, you know, Dr. T. was kind of freaked out by the bullfrogs."

"How come?" Mom asked.

"They're huge, with huge appetites! They'll eat everything and any-thing!"

"It's a good thing there aren't any around here," Dad kidded. "You'd have to duke it out over those mashed potatoes!"

Jackson set his fork down. With two fists on the table, he told them, "The bullfrogs take over habitat, big-time. When they move into a marsh, other amphibian species don't do so well. They just can't compete. The bullfrogs are new here. Sort of invaders."

"So, they're worse than the freaky frogs with extra legs?" Dad asked.

"I'm not really sure. The bullfrogs are carriers for chytrid fungus. And it turns out the fungus that's causing…" Jackson tilted his head and paused, thinking. "Malformations in frogs. That's doing way worse things."

Dad's eyebrows raised. "Worse things than multiple or missing legs?"

"Oh, yeah," Jackson answered. "Mass extinctions of a lot of frog species—all over the world."

There was quiet for a moment, everyone in their own thoughts. Jackson had stopped eating, then he said, "So the Atrazine, that weed killer, is causing the sex change thing, and the fungus is killing off whole species."

Mom and Dad looked at each other. "You sound like a real scientist," Mom said.

"A herpetologist," Jackson told them.

"So, what do you think is worse, the herbicides—what did you call it?"

"Atrazine."

So, Atrazine and pollution or the bullfrogs and the fungus?" Mom asked.

"I don't really know which one is worse, but I do know what's scaring Dr. T. the most."

Mom and Dad waited for him to continue. "Not knowing." he said.

"Not knowing what?" asked Dad.

"Not knowing a cause," Jackson answered. "You can't do anything about a problem if you don't know its cause. People are taking frogs from the wild, raising them in labs, and trying to help them get resistant to the fungus. But, remember the frogs with tails?"

Mom and Dad nodded.

Jackson continued, "They don't know what's causing that, yet."

"It's a wonder there are any frogs left in the world," Mom said.

Jackson told them about the frog chorus and the restaurant ideas. As hungry as he was, he talked non-stop between bites.

"This kind of reminds me of the, what did he call that frog? Ah, yes. *The Celebrated Frog of Calavaras County*," Dad said.

Jackson was half out of his seat, about to ask permission to leave the table, but that brought him back down. "Where's that?"

"You remember reading anything by Mark Twain?" Mom asked, as she began stacking their plates.

"You mean Tom Sawyer and Huck Finn?"

"The same," Dad answered. "But this is one of his short stories."

Jackson pushed his plate towards Mom, then crossed his arms on the table and leaned in. "So why did they celebrate a frog? What was so special about him?"

"Well, in this case, I think it means he was admired, famous," Dad said, waiting for the question he knew was coming.

"Famous for what?" Jackson's eyes got big. "Oh! Was he a freaky frog?"

Dad laughed. "Well, it's really the story of a story teller."

Jackson scratched his head. "Huh? What about the frog?"

"Well, this man was in the habit of betting. He would bet on anything. The weather, horse races, whether someone was going to die or get well, even whether a bug crossing the road would make it to the other side. What did he call that bug, Hon?"

Mom shook her head and Jackson put his head between his hands. "Dad! The frog!"

Mom grinned. "I don't remember the bug, but yes, he'd sure bet on all kinds of animals." She came back to the table and sat with them. "And as I recall, if he couldn't get anyone to take his bet on the other side, he'd switch sides."

"Jackson sat up straight and took a deep breath. "Dad! What about the famous frog?" He could see Mom and Dad were enjoying this.

"Yes, the *celebrated* frog."

Jackson threw his forehead down onto his arms, which made Dad laugh out loud. "Well, this betting man had a frog. He spent a lot of time teaching it to jump."

"You don't have to teach a frog to jump! "

Dad raised his hands in the air beside his head. "Hey, I'm just repeating Mark Twain's story. So, he bet his frog against any oncomer."

"Did he always win?"

Mom answered, "Yes, until..." She looked at Dad, who continued.

"One day, he ran into a stranger in town. The stranger asked him what he had in the box he was carrying." Dad stopped.

"It was the frog!"

"Oh, you've heard this one," Dad teased.

This time Jackson just stared, his eyes stretched wide open.

"All right, all right," Dad said. "Of course, the frog owner told the man his frog could beat any other in Calavaras County. He proposed a bet right there on the spot. When the man told him he would take the bet if he had a frog of his own, the frog owner asked him to hold his box and he would go get another one."

"Did he?"

"Sure, he had to if he wanted the bet. But while he was gone, the stranger poured buckshot into the frog's mouth. What do you suppose that did?"

"Kill it?"

"No, but that frog didn't do much hopping after that."

Jackson moaned. "I guess he lost the race."

"Yes, I think that pretty much ended his career" Dad answered.

"Oh, speaking of careers…" Jackson started. "Could I go with Dr. T. and the team again tomorrow? They're working longer than they originally planned."

"If that's the way you want to spend your Saturday, it's fine with me," said Dad.

Jackson looked at Mom, who said, "I don't mind, so long as you find time for your chores. And who's career are we talking about?"

"Mine. I hope." He paused. "Do you think I could be a real herpetologist? Like Dr. T.?"

Mom answered, "I don't see why not. It looks like you've got a pretty good start."

Rising, Jackson said, "Thanks! I'm going to call Raina and see if her mom is letting her go."

"Right after you finish clearing the table, Dr. McDowell!" Mom said.

Chapter 18

Frog Watchers

THE following day, everyone on the team caught at least one bullfrog. They were also netting tadpoles. "I thought everyone would be more excited," Jackson told Raina, at the end of the day. "I was sure excited when I caught mine."

On the drive home, Jackson's mood, in fact, everyone's mood was subdued. "I'm half sad it's ending, but I'm glad, too. I don't really know why."

Dr. Thomson had a suggestion. "Maybe, if you're like me, you need some time to digest it all. Mull it over. And we now have a great deal of work to do."

"Yeah, paper work," Bill said. "We're going to miss you guys," he told the kids, and everyone agreed. Some even gave the kids their e-mail addresses, to keep in touch.

The rest of the summer passed quickly, but the week before school started, Jackson's family had a party to watch a new show on television. They invited Dr. Thomson, Bill and Stacy and Mr. Dorr. Of course, Raina and her mom were there, and quite a few friends from school, particularly students from Jackson's science class.

But CK wasn't there. The Frog Rap had been a huge success in Faraday and had gone viral on the internet. When an offer was extended to CK for a small part in a television sitcom, his family moved to California. Jackson's family had invited friends to watch the first episode together. "I wonder if he's eating frogs' legs." Raina asked Jackson.

There was some discussion about frogs, of course, with so many of Jackson's "frog friends" convening. Jackson and Raina told everyone the high points of their week surveying.

"So," asked Mr. Dorr. "Is the creek better off now than when the team first surveyed it?"

"Well, the creek is cleaner, less algae than when the ranch was there." Jackson explained. Dr. T. says there are fewer freaky frogs. I haven't seen any more out there with more than four legs."

Dr. Thomson confirmed that signs were improving for a healthy environment for the frogs, as well as people in the area. "But those bullfrogs–taking over habitat, and possibly increasing the spread of a deadly virus, will be competition for the native frogs in and around Faraday. They could eventually stress their populations."

"I've been looking for ways I can help frogs," Jackson said.

"And what have you come up with? Mr. Dorr asked.

"I can be a frog watcher. Well, any of us can be."

"That's easy for you to say," joked their friend Trish. "You live on a creek."

"There are frogs all over, Jackson told her. "In your backyard or a ditch. In any low place, or place where water puddles. Really. You just need to go out at dusk or after dark and listen. Then, if you register with Frog Watch USA, you can report what you heard on the data base. It's not year-round. Only from February through August."

"I wouldn't know a bullfrog from a Kermit frog," Trish answered, getting a laugh from everyone.

"Oh, they'll train you. Most of the training sessions are in March, so we missed them. And there weren't any in our area, anyway. But we can still train online."

Several responses came at once. "Cool!"

Let's do it!"

"Where do I sign up?"

Dr. Thomson answered that one: "I think we can arrange a live training right here, in Faraday, if we could just come up with some interested volunteers," he joked.

At that, there were many enthusiastic responses.

Jackson smiled as he watched his teacher interact with the students. *How does he do it?* He wondered. He had to raise his voice to speak. "The other thing I think we can do is have a Save the Frogs Day." Everyone wanted to talk at once. "Can we, Dr. T.?" someone asked.

"What would we have to do?" asked Marcos, just as his twin Miguel, always in sync with his brother, asked, "Where would we have it?"

Mr. Dorr stood and put his hands up in front of him. "Whoa! Jackson, tell us a little about your idea."

"Well, it's not really my idea. Save the Frogs has been doing it for about ten years. People in a lot of countries volunteer and hold Save the Frog Day in different places, like schools and museums. It's always the last Saturday in April."

"Aw, man! We missed that, too!" someone called.

"Wait a minute, wait a minute! This sounds like an undertaking that will take some planning time–IF we decide to tackle it," Mr. Dorr told them.

"Oh, we have to!" said two people at once.

"So, Jackson, what would we have to do?" Mr. Dorr asked.

"Yeah," said Miranda. "Do you really think kids can do it? I'd like to help save the frogs."

There was a chorus of "Me, too!"

Jackson looked at Mr. Dorr. "Go on, Jackson. This is your baby."

"Save the Frogs will help you with ideas. But I have one of my own." The group waited, for once, not shouting out. "We could have a frog jumping contest."

The group's restraint was short lived. Questions and comments shot out like bullets.

"How far does a frog jump?"

"How would that help the frogs?"

"Where would we hold it?"

"Would frogs even want to race?"

"Sure they would! Frogs love to jump," Denise answered. "We could charge an entry fee and donate the money to Help Save the Frogs."

"That's what I was thinking," said Jackson.

"And take up a collection from the people who come to watch." Trish suggested.

"We'll write up a proposal and give it to Mr. Brewer. I bet he'll let us do it in the gym," Mr. Dorr said, as he patted Jackson's shoulder. "We've got lots of time, but it will pass quickly. Looks like we've got a core planning committee right here!"

There were lots of ideas bantered about. "We could sell Hoppy Meals to earn more money," Barry said. "Just how far can a frog hop, anyway?"

All eyes turned to Jackson.

"Well, I did some research. There's a famous contest, the Calaveras County Jumping Frog Jubilee. I think it's based on a story by Mark Twain. The contestants get three jumps. The world record is held by Rosie the Ribeter, a bullfrog. In 1986 she jumped more than twenty-one feet."

Jackson's dad spoke up. "Hey, I think it's just about time for CK's big debut."

Mrs. McDowell turned on the television. CK's show was a hit with the kids. He was billed by his real name, Christopher Kim. Everyone agreed he had a future in Hollywood. Someone said, "Who knew a kid like CK would become so popular?"

But then, look at me, Jackson thought. *When I first came to Faraday, I had no friends. I was just a dumb kid. Now I'm a herpetologist. I'm the Frogman!*

* * *

Raina and Jackson continued to explore the creek, keeping a lookout for freaky frogs.

Each night when he went to bed, Jackson lay listening to the night sounds. He had learned to recognize quite a few frog sounds. Of course, this time of year was breeding season, so a lot of the night noises, and even some daytime noises, were calls to repel males and attract females as potential mates. He didn't wish the frogs ill, of course, but his favorite was the alarm call, two to three calls. He'd learned that one on his own, when he approached frogs by the creek and witnessed the call, then splash.

Every night, as he lay listening, Jackson wondered when he would hear the "Giga rummm rummm. Giga rummm rummm," that would tell him the bullfrogs had arrived at his neck of the creek. Before drifting off to sleep, Jackson often shined his flashlight into the habitat next to his bed and watched the tailed frog. He was certain now. *By the time I finish college, there will still be plenty of work for herpetologists like me. I'll teach kids, just like Dr. T. teaches me. Except I'll be Dr. J.*

UV Rap

Vitamin D's a good thing. We get it from the sun.
But too much sun can harm you, if your tan gets overdone.
The Ultraviolet rays, (UV rays, for short)
Can really cause you trouble, and so we will exhort…
Use Sunscreen! Use Sunscreen!
The ozone can protect us, it keeps the UVs out
But holes are being 'eaten,' by fossil fuels, no doubt.
And so the poor amphibians, like frog and salamander
Are suffer-ing at humans' hand, we've really raised their dander.
They live on land and water, and they surely do absorb
Whatever be-comes toxic, when hit by that big orb.
Use sunscreen! Use sunscreen!
They have no sunscreen, shades, or hats,
And now, they're turning freaky.
So, take their cue for a healthy you:
Protection's cool, not geeky!

Freaky Frogs Glossary

abnormality- not normal, not usual, not typical

absorb- to suck up or soak up

acai [ah-sigh-ee]- berry from a palm native to South and Central America, thought to be good for health

affirmative- agreement with a statement or request

aquatic- related to water; a plant or animal living or growing in water

aquifer- an underground formation containing water; may supply water for wells or springs, either hollow, or of porous rock, gravel or sand where water can flow through its pores

amphibian- a cold- blooded animal that can live on both land and in water; having both gills and lungs

apparent- clearly or easily seen

anomaly- irregular or abnormal; different from the usual

astute- mentally sharp; smart

bacteria- plural of bacterium; one-celled organism often involved in infectious diseases

biology- scientific study of life forms and how they grow

buckshot- lead pellet ammunition for shotguns

captive- one who is enslaved, imprisoned, or locked up

Celsius- measurement of temperature with the freezing point of water defined as 0 degrees and the boiling point as 100 degrees; Celsius is used by most countries of the world, with the exception of the United States, Belize, and the Cayman Islands.

chronicles- record of events; history

city slicker- a person raised in the city and accustomed to life there.

clarify- make clear

clone- (noun) an organism that duplicates or imitates, or closely resembles another; (verb) to reproduce an exact copy of an organism artificially, or without sex

commentary- explanation or record of events

concoction- mixture of two or more ingredients

conduit- a tube to protect electrical wiring

consecutive- following one another in order, without interruption

consequence- effect or result of something that happened before

contaminant- (noun) something that makes impure, polluted, unclean, or unusable

contaminate (verb)- the act of making impure, polluted, unclean, or unusable

controversial- debatable; may cause disagreement

convene- come together for a meeting

culvert- drain or ditch running along a roadway, or under the road

dander- loose scales formed on the skin and shed from the coat or feathers of various animals; anger or temper

data- plural of datum; facts, statistics or items of information

dawn on- receive a new idea; understand

demeanor- outward behavior, a body posture that might indicate a person's feelings or attitude

dexterous- clever, quick or skillful use of hands or body

digits- fingers or toes; also, Arabic numerals 1-9 and 0

discreet- using good judgment in conduct or speech; being silent about a sensitive subject dubious- doubtful, questionable, uncertain, unsure

DNA- deoxyribonucleic acid; formation of the chromosome that carries genes which identify individuals or characteristics of an individual

edibles- eatables; food

enhanced- increased, elevated, improved

epidermis- outermost layer of skin

exhort- to warn or strongly advise

exotic- not native; introduced from another area

exuberance- being full of energy, excitement, cheerfulness

Fahrenheit- measure of temperature where the freezing point of water is set at 32 degrees and the boiling point at 212 degrees. Fahrenheit is used officially in the United States, Belize, and the Cayman Islands only.

Far-fetched- unlikely, doubtful, unbelievable or unthinkable

fungi- plural of fungus; organisms including mushrooms and mildew that live by decomposing or absorbing organic material they live in or on. Fungi cannot make their own food.

grad students- graduate students; students who have completed four years of college, have a bachelor's degree and are working on advanced degrees

greenhouse gases- gases which absorb solar radiation, and cause warming of the atmosphere

habitat- natural environment of an organism. Containers sold in pet stores are also called habitats.

herbicide- a substance used to kill plants, usually weeds

herps- reptiles and amphibians

herpetologist- zoologist who studies or specializes in reptiles and amphibians

hydrologist- scientist who studies or specializes in water

hypothesis- a suggestion made on the basis of limited evidence as a starting point for further investigation. A hypothesis is not a final conclusion. It will be altered as further evidence is discovered.

indicator species- plant or animal that is usually the first to be affected by harmful environmental conditions

initiate- begin, or start

lethargic- drowsy, dull, or lacking energy

linguist- person who is skilled in language

lobby- noun: main entryway of a building; verb: seek to pressure or convince of a certain opinion or action

manifestation- act of showing something in a clear and understandable way

mate- noun: one of a pair; verb: to breed or produce offspring

mesmerize- hypnotize or fascinate

mosey- wander leisurely or strol; walk slowly

mournful- gloomy, sad

mull- think about carefully; ponder

murmur- a low, continuous sound

nitrates- naturally occurring chemicals that are left after the breakdown or decomposition of animal or human waste;

nocturnal- active at night, resting during daylight hours

optional- voluntary, not required

organism- an individual living plant or animal or single-cell life form

observant- quick to notice; carefully watches

occurred- happened

orb- circle or sphere; a heavenly body, such as the sun

ozone layer- gaseous layer which absorbs ultraviolet light in the upper atmosphere, but is a pollutant close to the earth's surface

parasites- organism which lives on a plant or animal of a different species from which it gets its nutrients; an organism which lives off another organism

perching- settling or resting, often in a raised location

percolate- to pass through a porous substance; filter, ooze or trickle

permeable- a material that lets liquid or gas pass through it

phenomenon- a fact or happening that can be observed

polarized glasses- glasses designed to filter out glare; glasses labeled *UV protection* filter out. blue or ultraviolet radiation that is harmful to the eyes **porous**- full of tiny holes that water can pour through

potential- possibility of something good in the future

practical- operating in a sensible way

pursed- lips pressed together

ponder- think about carefully

potential- possible

quest- mission or adventure in search of something

quick study- someone who catches on or learns quickly

radiant- sending out rays of light or energy, shining

reluctant- unwilling or not wanting to do something

renoun- fame, celebrity

repel- push back or away; hold off

riparian- area next to a body of water; area where water runs into a body of water

reverie- daydream, pleasant thoughts

siege- surround, cut off or block

sentinel- person or animal that stands and gives warning of impending danger

septic tank- underground chamber that receives waste and wastewater from a house

sheepish- embarrassed or bashful

skew- distorts or misrepresent

squeamish- easily made to feel sick, faint or disgusted

sophisticated- having knowledge and experience of the world; advanced or complicated

species- group of plants or animals which have the same characteristics

SPF- Sun Protection Factor is the measurement of how well a lotion or cream blocks out harmful UV radiation. Generally, the greater the SPF, the greater the protection.

stealthily- secretly or in a sneaky way

surplus- more than enough, extra

swell- expand, get bigger; also, a slow movement of the sea, a rolling wave

tack- saddle, bridle and equipment required for riding a horse; also means to change direction of a boat in a zigzag pattern; also, a sharp, short nail

terrarium- glass container for growing plants; May be used as a vivarium, or living space, for animals

toxic- poisonous

trajectory- path or course

tuatara- large, lizard like reptile, native to New Zealand
    universal- affecting or concerning all or every

UV- ultraviolet light, harmful to unprotected skin and eyes

vent- opening or outlet

vertebrate- animal having an internal skeleton and backbone; mammal, bird, reptile, amphibian and fish

vibrant- lively, energetic, stimulating

virus- organism which grows within cells of plants, bacteria and animals; disease caused by a virus

witness- v. see an event; n. a person who sees an event

wrinkle- problem; also, crease in the skin or fabric

zoology- study of animals

The Frog Jokes

What kind of footwear does a fashionable frog wear? Open-toad shoes

What's green and hops? A frog; What's red and hops? A very angry frog;

What's red, hops and is dangerous? An angry frog with a hand grenade.

Why are frogs such liars? They're amphibians.

What's a frog's favorite car? The Beetle

Why did all the frogs croak after dinner? They ate the poison dessert.

What did the frog say when he found a piece of paper? "Rippit. Rippit."

A frog was bored so he decided to see a fortune teller. The lady took his flipper in her hand and traced a line with her index finger. "I'm afraid you have a short lifeline. But the good news is, very soon, you will meet a beautiful young woman." "Oh, great," said the frog. "When and where?" "Next week, in her biology class."

Why are frogs so happy? They can eat whatever bugs them.

What's a frog's favorite restaurant? I Hop.

What has more lives than a cat? A frog. He croaks every night.

What happens if a frog's parking meter expires? He gets toad.

How can you tell if a frog has no ears? Yell "Free flies!" and he doesn't come.

One day a baby frog asked his mother, "Who's smarter, chickens or frogs?"

"Frogs, of course," she answered. "How do you know?" asked the baby. "Have you ever heard of Kentucky fried frog?"

What did the frog driver say to the frog hitchhiker? "Hop in!"

What's green and goes one hundred miles an hour? A frog in a blender.

Why couldn't the snake talk? He had a frog in his throat.

What's a frog's favorite music? Hip Hop

Why do frogs have webbed feet? To stamp out forest fires

What do Scottish frogs play? Hop Scotch

A Message from the Author

FROG species around the world are in decline. Over two hundred species are extinct and one hundred more are expected to disappear in the next century. Frogs not only play an important role in the food web, they are important indicator species, giving the first warning when something goes wrong in the environment.

You can help. To become a frog watcher, contact The American Association of Zoos and Aquariums, Frogwatch@aza.org. To host a Save the Frogs Day, contact SavetheFrogs.com

In a study by Dr. Krista McCoy, University of Florida School of Natural Resources and the Environment, it was determined that environmental stress from suburban development did not have as great an impact on amphibians as farm related activities. According to Dr. Lou Guillette, professor of zoology, "As you increase agriculture, you have an increasing number of abnormalities."

To see the report, go to www.Scienceagogo.com. In the search bar, enter *Farmlands too toxic for amphibians.*

Then God said, "Let us make mankind in our image, in our likeness, so that they may rule over the fish in the sea and the birds in the sky, over the livestock and all the wild animals, and over all the creatures that move along the ground."

Genesis 1:26 NIV

Made in USA - Crawfordsville, IN
68042_9781734050004
01.19.2021 0545